CW01661980

Iain M

THE BOY WITH THE THORN IN HIS SIDE

This edition first published in paperback by
Michael Terence Publishing in 2022
www.mtp.agency

ISBN 9781800944190

Cover image
courtesy of Sean Ballie

Michael Terence
Publishing

Big thanks to Sean Ballie for the photography.

*Peter Callan for the help with the final edit
and for pointing out my glaring mistakes.*

Everyone at Fir Park, old and new.

To all those trudging the road of Happy Destiny.

Contents

Prologue

He sat there smugly, an aura of superiority surrounding him as the therapist looked over his glasses asking him question after question. Frankie batted the answers back to him swiftly saying nothing while talking constantly, feeling he had the upper hand as though his working-class background and life experience somehow gave him the edge over his middle-class interrogator, like he knew something this guy didn't. A position of comfort he had learnt at school over the middle classes who seemed somehow weaker and lower in the pecking order. A childish survival kit he should have let go of long ago but somehow served him well in his world. The session seemed to drag on and he left the tiny room feeling another box was ticked until he sat there again next week playing the role he knew only too well as the therapist tried to untangle him. Frankie drove in silence, no music to drown out his thoughts and he wondered how he had ended up here. 29 years of age, seeing a therapist, self-help books and probation officers all part of his weekly routine though he never seen himself as that fucked up before, well not compared to half the people he grew up with. He thought the anxiety and anger were just par for the course when you had smoked a lot of dope, been through the rave thing and liked a drink. Surely, he was no different to the rest? He let go of the thought as he pulled up outside his flat, climbing the stairs to his safe haven a place where he could rest his body and calm his mind down to a riot. Although he hadn't worked in weeks now, he felt constantly exhausted and lay on top of his bed with sleep coming quickly. Rest never came though. His body was still but he knew as soon as he stepped through the door to dream world the fight was on. A world where he was always running, chased by someone, fighting someone off who meant him harm. He woke suddenly and sharply in the usual frightened state his body dampened with the familiar sweat of doing 12 rounds in his sleep. Awake to fight another day. He got up and went to the bathroom, emptying his bladder, washed his face and looked at his watch. It was still only 6.30pm. He lit a cigarette as he opened the kitchen window wide to let the smoke sneak out as he looked at the street below as the sun nipped his eyes.

Frankie felt that life had dealt him a poor hand and wished he could feel free again, free of his own thoughts free of the anxiety that had plagued him for too long, he thought back to a time before all this, before drugs, when a night out wasn't a bender. A time when he was an optimistic teenager. A teenager who had just started his peering into the adult world in wonder. BMX bikes had been his previous source of excitement, almost obsession but the excitement had quickly ended and he was seeking new thrills, new ways to get his blood pumping and his mind occupied. He had always liked music but then it seemed to be far more important to him in such tribal times it was so important to belong to the right group, he hated the way the modern romantic lot dressed so like girls and the punks were so scruffy and scary looking. Skinheads could be cool the ones who had the right clothes not just shaved heads and boots and Two Tone was great to listen too so he started buying records as often as he could afford and he adopted the look of the Fred Perry, levis jeans and Harrington jacket though he wasn't allowed a close crop he did get a "number 3 cut" which was all his Mum would allow and she still protested that he looked like a convict though he loved it. He felt the bees' knees as he walked down the street in any new clothes and the feeling of excitement had followed him through his whole life. It could make or break how he felt about himself any given day. At school if he was wearing his chosen outfit, he felt like he was shining. On other days or he felt like he could die of embarrassment as he was forced to leave the house in his Mums chosen attire. Trousers he felt were flares in a time of drainpipes. As life moved on so did fashion and Frankie followed suit always with one eye on what was happening as he adopted the look of the casual and the hunt for labels all too costly for the average joe which only belonged to him and his tribe. Every new item inflating his self-esteem to the point of arrogance at times. He was free though and life was feeling good as weekends moved from drinking cider in the woods at weekends during his teenage years to the bright lights and thumping sounds in local clubs and massive raves all over the country. But where had it all gone wrong for him? He watched the guys he grew up with, drank with even, begin to grow up round about him and begin to get good jobs, decent earners and girlfriends and settle into the mundane with plans of marriage and children as he floated aimlessly through life choosing his company in those who lived like he did. He had little ambition and for a guy who cared about everything at the same time cared about nothing. Was there something wrong with him or was he just different from the rest? Maybe a bit of both.

1

The boy with the thorn in his :

That night was spend staring at the TV constantly flicking through channels searching for something to hold his attention as he smoked cigarette after cigarette between never ending cups of coffee as he waited on the next day arriving. Pay day would come and his bank account would be full once more, a wage unearned which kept coming every month as long as he kept the sick lines coming.

He felt high on anticipation as he woke that Friday knowing today would be different. The last few days dragged on with no money and living on cornflakes and coffee. The last packet of cigarettes he had to ration to see him through. Frankie showered quickly, got dressed and was on the street in jig time, marching down the town to the hustle and bustle he needed, enjoying the certain feeling as he joined the queue at the ATM. He whistled the tune to "PRETTY GREEN" as the notes were fed into his palm from the machine stuffing them into his wallet knowing all would be well for today at least.

His life seemed to shift forward over the next day or so in different speeds as though he was being controlled remotely or working on auto pilot, he remembered the initial hour in the pub as he consumed the first few drinks he had longed for the days before and his world slowed down to a place of peace where he glowed like the kids in the old Ready Brek adverts. Then he blinked and it was midnight and he was in a Taxi gliding through the scheme he grew up in as he scanned for lights on in the usual addresses where parties were a plenty and friendship seemed strong under the alcohol haze. It then seemed like he blinked and was putting the key in his own door, home after a 48 hour stretch where he had little recollection of where he had been or who he had been with. It was like looking through a photo album where half the pictures were lost and some of the faces he didn't recognise. He was unsure if the faces in his mind's eye were friends or enemies. If he had laughed with them or fought with them, he just couldn't be sure. It puzzled Frankie at this point as the booze still pumped through his veins keeping him calm but this puzzled feeling would turn to fear…no not fear much more than fear. Terror. It would turn to terror as he awoke from a well needed sleep and the prospect made Frankie shudder. He entered his flat picking up the last two days mail and locked the door behind him removing the key to give the impression of an empty house to onlookers from outside. He went into the kitchen and removed the half-drunk bottle of cheap wine from the inside pocket off his jacket and placed it on the window ledge as he began to stick three skins together in an attempt to build a joint. One last charge before he slept and would awake to face himself again, a joint that would help to numb his dreams and anesthetise him.

He slept in peace and had no memory of his dreams though woke with the usual damp sweat on his body, as the world came back into focus, he felt drained, a body deprived of any nutrition and mind confused over recent days events and a soul with a need for something to save him…was it love he craved to complete him and take away this longing he couldn't shake? Had growing up with the madness of his Father left a void in him somehow. He felt a constant need he had tried to satisfy his whole life but could only dampen the feeling temporarily with drink or drugs as though the chemicals pumping through his bloodstream slowed down his mind and gave him rest bite from himself. He checked his mobile phone for evidence of drunken phone calls to God knows who and emptied his jeans pockets to see how much cash he had left. No cash bar a few coins but better still no evidence of him drinking and dialling. He had a strange habit of phoning ex-girlfriends or females from his past in any form when he was out of it. At times the phone calls had the desired effect and got him a bed for the night but at other times he had to face the shame the next day as he couldn't remember what kind of response he got. Best of it is some of the lassies were just clocking in with the past for a night and fulfilled his needs but others he wouldn't even say hello to when he was sober never mind phone them up. This off the wall behaviour all added to his state of mind when sober and his constant bouts of anxiety and self-loathing all taking place inside him as he strolled through the town as though he owned the place. There were times where he had let his guard down a bit and tried to express some of these mixed feelings and emotions to the therapist the Doctor had sent him to but the guy just looked at him with an even more puzzled look as he attempted to explain feeling full of self-loathing while you were sure you hovered above the world as though you were somehow superior. The guys puzzled looks only made him feel judged and caused him to clam up again to the confinement of his own inner world. A world where he let nobody in but fought demons daily in his dreams and tried to keep up the pretence that he was sorted and a free spirit self-assured to the core. You couldn't mark him with a hatchet his mate used to say as Frankie smiled back easily fooling the world.

Today he felt different though, not better or worse but different. As though he needn't play the mind games too long with himself trying to untangle the recent bender like he normally did, did he offend anyone? Were they coming after him? Whoever they might be, the polis, somebody's big brother, did he owe anyone an apology, was there any money owed? Frankie felt like there was some feeling a chapter was ending and a new day would dawn. A feeling like what would be would be and the wheels had been set in motion and his fate had been sealed. It was beginning to feel like the baw was burst and he needed to pick a new game to play. A fate he was unsure of but knew change was looming. His jailer would come to lock him up or turn the key to free him but Frankie knew a change was coming where things would never be the same again. This feeling provided him with some reassurance and fear at the same time as though he knew but didn't want to look. Like waking up with a sore face throbbing but you're scared to look in the mirror to see the extent of the damage and choose to stay blissfully unaware as the throb worsens reminding you it is there.

The next few days passed with Frankie rarely leaving the

flat, bar the usual tip to the local shop for necessities. He lay about fairly calm with the feeling that "they" were coming to get him having left him pretty quickly after his last drink. At times the terror had been unbearable and had subsided to mild panic in a few days but the feeling of impending doom had stuck to him for a week before. He was thankful that he had shaken it off fairly quickly on this occasion, usually an indication that within the patches of memory loss there had been nothing to write home about or deep inside he would know.

Thursday came as it did every week and Frankie again sat in from of the therapist. It was his third appointment with this Mr Bradshaw and he was still not really sure of what was going on here and felt it highly unlikely that this guy could help him or even if he needed help at all? Did he attend these places to please others? His work, his Doctor? Who knows? Frankie felt a little more focussed today and was firing a few questions of his own at Mr Bradshaw. It was explained that the process they were hoping to explore was based on Psychodynamic Therapy where by untangling his past particularly childhood it may give insight into how he felt today. Frankie focussed on the Psycho bit of the word Psychodynamic and felt a wave of panic as though he was being labelled a psycho. Did this guy Bradshaw think he was a psycho? Frankie's scheme mentality soon provided him with the reassurance that he would easily smash this guy if he said anything wide.

Mr Bradshaw began asking Frankie about his childhood as though some beast had been touching him under the covers at night but Frankie thought he would play along and at least try to be open minded. He thought back to his earliest memory an image of himself with dungarees and a blonde bowl cut walking in front of his mother on reins the whole family smiling on a Blackpool holiday. He couldn't be sure though if this was a memory or just a photograph, he had seen many times as he must been about three in the picture and you couldn't remember that far back, could you? He saw other images in his mind, happy times of him riding a new bike, a Tomahawk the bike he imagined he was part of the "California Highway Patrol" on as he and his mates rode round the scheme. His early memories seemed fond with flashes of holidays in cold English seaside towns, playing with Action Men and Star Wars figures, twenty-five a side football matches and sailing boats in the pond of the local park. He felt safe as a wean, happy with no real concerns in life. He was a good boy who did his best at school though never top of the class, certainly never a dunce. He got on with everyone at Primary School but had the odd scrap like most boys did. Surley none of this stuff marked him in any great way? As though Mr Bradshaw could read his mind, he nodded in the affirmative encouraging him to keep talking.

Frankie scoured his mind for something negative to work with to give this guy what he wanted and tried to express that the only time he felt on the fringes of anything was in the hot July summers of Marching season when it seemed like every weekend the streets of the scheme filled with orange sashes and flutes as the parades warmed up for the big day in Ireland on the

12th. Big base drums raining thunderous roars up the narrow streets as the masses followed. Frankie always felt that during this time he was shunned a little and some who were normally his best mates would now pass him with merely an acknowledging nod as though they didn't want to be seen with him. It was clear to him now but the young Frankie didn't know that although not a catholic himself half his family were of the catholic faith and this labelled him a Fenian. Particularly with the name being Francis. He never knew then what a Fenian was then but he knew he didn't want to be one. As Frankie's family were mixed, he was never brought up with religion of any kind and as a wee boy he didn't understand it and it all seemed unfair and confusing to him how he could be cast out for no reason. A feeling of being on the outside looking in followed him at times after that first July and he viewed the Orange Men with great caution thereafter. The sight of the orange sash heightened his senses from that day on.

He caught Mr Bradshaw almost smirking at one point as Frankie relayed the stories of his childhood memories as though he was laughing at Frankie internally or was, he just telling him he understood? Either way Frankie clamed up a little and felt like a mug for opening up to him in the first place. It seemed Bradshaw recognised this as his demeaner suddenly changed into counsellor mode again as he got serious again asking Frankie more questions in a softer fashion almost relaxing Frankie again.

His mind drifted back to when he was a boy as though inside a lens looking at his surroundings as others around him seemed connected. Telepathically in tune and Frankie was still turning the knob looking for the frequency but always had the wee bit of static in the air making him uneasy as the rest seemed content floating in a groove he could never find. He though about his first group of friends after they had finished playing with toys but not quite hit puberty yet. An awkward age where you were trying to find your feet in the world. Luckily for them they grew up in an era where you picked your tribe. He idolised Madness, The Specials, Bad Manners and his classmate who did the same instantly bonded together leaving childhood behind and suddenly the quest to become cool was on. Clothes and hairstyles now mattered but not quite girls yet that would come later. He bonded with these boys laughing constantly, singing, mimicking their hero's during school. Rick from The Young Ones, Vivian even, laughing their heads off all day. Watching VHS films at home, Quadrophenia, The Wanderers, First Blood. This was a time of exploration almost dipping your toe into the adult world but still the mind and body of a wee boy. A time Frankie looked back on with fond memories and also sadness. As quickly as these bonds were made, they were broken by simple geography. As Primary School ended the group moved onto different secondary schools through different choices and religions and he rarely seen them thereafter and when he did it was like they were back to being casual acquaintances again as though they were only meant to be there for that short chapter not the whole story and they each understood this.

With Secondary School looming Frankie felt all alone again.

2

My old man

The teenage group fuelled on cheap wine and cider had laughed and sung their way through a cold February night in Lanarkshire. This was normal entertainment for these thirteen- and fourteen-year-olds like their older Brothers and Sisters had done before them. One day they would graduate to the comfort of the warm pubs and clubs. Until then the graveyard would have to do.

This was a time where oblivion was something to be proud of and mayhem encouraged. All to have taken place before the 11pm curfew where these youngsters would need to present themselves in front of waiting parents like choir boys who done no wrong. It was a skill learnt quickly and most mastered the art with ease. Fooling the parents who would spend the biggest chunk of their weekend under the influence. A role model who would pave the way to a life of drunkenness and unfulfilled potential branding their kids black sheep and wondering what went wrong?

Frankie and his young friends had walked from the dark graveyard singing football songs with arms around each other's shoulders, the alcohol making the friendship seem like a Brotherhood. The bright lights of the town having a sobering effect on them as they once more came into their reality and the 11pm curfew pending. Some of these kids could snap out of the drunken haze like a hypnotist clicking his fingers and bringing them back into the room. Safe to go home with their reputation as model children intact. Frankie always struggled with this, the booze seemed to affect him differently. It seemed to possess him somehow and there was no kidding with it. His eyes bloodshot red and his body loose under the effect of the cheap wine and cider. He was free though, free of any troubles, he was at one with the world. He was equal to all. The curfew imposed by his tyrannical father was the only dampener on these nights. He knew there would be a price to pay for having fun.

The small group parted ways as they headed home to face the music, most sleeping soundly that night passing the parental test with flying colours. This was rarely the case for Frankie. He had to walk the gauntlet through his Fathers anger and simmering drunken rage. He couldn't quite put his finger on it but he always felt his old man hated him for some reason. Like his presence was enough just to anger him. Frankie hated his father even as a teenager, wished him dead at times. Strangely there was still a part of him longed for some attention from him, a connection that was just never there. Frankie was like the ships cat who got booted every time his father was pissed off. An object used to focus his father's pain on. You only ever got his father two ways, drunk and volatile or sober and irritable. He was best avoided in both conditions. A Tyrant and a bully.

Frankie took a deep breath and entered the family home via the back door trying to compose himself and play the innocent. He was bang on 11pm so knew he was ok on that front but now he had to navigate his father's mood and if he could pass the sobriety test. He was so afraid he almost giggled in laughter. He composed himself again and went to the fridge to have a fake look inside in an attempt to appear normal before he entered the living room. He closed the fridge door and walked into the living room nodding at his father confirming he was home safe. He felt the energy instantly as he entered the room, his father's side glance almost piercing him. He sat in his usual armchair pot-bellied with hands like shovels making the silver tanker in his hand appear like a thimble. Frankie attempted the slow composed walk up to his room where he would fake sleep until it came and awake tomorrow to safety once more. It was not to be however as soon as his first foot touched the bottom stair to safety, he heard the growl "Where ay you fuckin gaun?". The teenage Frankie stuttered a reply his brain unable to focus under the spotlight, "I'm, I'm …" His father leapt from the chair and bounced towards Frankie before he could reply properly. Like a silver backed gorilla on attack the beer belly and fists came towards him. His Father grabbed the scruff of his neck and throw him into the middle of the living room. He smelt the booze and cheap shitty aftershave with the flash of gold from his father's sovereign ring. He was now pinned to the wall by the throat as his father looked him in the eye with a mix of disgust and hatred. His father trying not to unload on him the rage seething. As the grip loosened on his throat, he relaxed for a split second just in time to feel the force of an almighty slap to the side of the head. Then another, then another. Frankie crouched over covering his acne covered face. He saw his father's tartan slipper come from below as he was booted on the forehead. Frankie exaggerated the scream he let out in an attempt to deter his attacker. The scream fell on deaf ears though and he was booted again and again between verbal that he was a useless cunt and he that he was not right in the fuckin heid. Frankie always found it ironic that the drunkest most insane person he knew would always call everyone out for being alcoholics and not right in the heed. Even as a teenager he knew there was some weird projection going on, something confusing, something insane. Frankie got up from the hedgehog position and ran to the stairs as his father made one more attempt to boot him missing by miles. He sprinted up the stairs and slammed his room door. The door closing was like he had armour at last. Armour from the punches, kicks, insults. He heard his father climb the stairs after him and Frankie jumped over his single bed. He pushed the full weight of the bed against the door barricading himself in, sitting against the bed his 10 stone adding to the weight. His Father banged and banged on the door, howling at Frankie that he was out of this house that he could fuck off. Minutes later his father went back downstairs the call of the tenant's lager stronger that the hatred for the young Frankie.

Frankie huddled in his bed as though the duvet would somehow protect him from further attack. The bed still firmly against the door giving him some added protection from his father. He was afraid to sleep but at the same time the world of dreams was more appealing to the reality he lived in.

The next morning Frankie awoke with a full bladder but

lay in bed eyes closed but still aware of the sunlight coming through his bedroom window. He held on as long as he could before he was forced to move the bed from the door and go back into the mad house to find the toilet.

Frankie safely locked in the bathroom. He pished then looked at his reflection in the bathroom mirror. He looked rough as toast. His hair standing on end, teenage acne covering his face mixed with bum fluff between the blemishes. These was a shadow under his right eye where his fathers had connected a blow the previous evening. Frankie flattened his hair with cold water in an attempt to improve how he looked. The acne added to his self-loathing with the taste of cheap wine still present in his mouth he scrubbed his tongue and teeth with his toothbrush trying to scrub away the evidence of the under ager drinking the night before. He left the bathroom bracing himself for further interrogation.

Just then his father passed him in the hallway. Fully clothed and looking fresh. Frankie put his head down in an attempt to appear invisible bracing himself for the possibility of some form of attack. His Father walked on towards the door and as he put his hand on the door handle before leaving, he turned to Frankie, "That us away out Son." "Will you be in for your dinner later?"

Frankie mumbled a reply. "Aye probably." His Father replied, "Alright son see you later on," before clicking his heals as he walked down the garden path to enjoy his day. His mother merely smiled while uttering, "See you later son." Frankie wondered if the smile she gave him was trying to say something to him in code? Was she even aware of the beating Frankie had received the previous evening? Did she care or was she just glad that she was not the recipient? His mother seemed dead behind the eyes at times as though she had given up on life and accepted her lot.

Frankie was confused, his anxiety spiking as he didn't know if his parents were playing games with him. Would he face his wrath again later or could his old man not remember last night? Frankie hadn't even served his apprenticeship in boozing and knew nothing about blackouts, memory loss, and remorse. He thought his further punishment may be on hold. He hoped he couldn't remember. It might just be better if he could get it over with whatever the next attack would be. The not knowing was always far worse than the actual beatings, it would almost be better if he was slapped punched and kicked every night rather than sporadically. Right now, he would live to fight another day and see how his luck played out.

3

Sunshine on Leith

Monday morning again and the pain at the side of his skull was like a vice crushing him. The familiar pain that followed him around. A pain he once thought a brain tumor it so extreme and mixed with his racing thoughts always trawling for the worst-case scenario. Frankie knew the pain though, an irritant caused by grinding his teeth each night and holding his jaw like a jockey's left hand as he attempted sleep.

He lit the first cigarette of the day before he even filled the kettle. He thought back to the session with Bradshaw and how he seemed to be trying to untangle his life and identify where things didn't quite go according to the grand plan. He thought of his first days at secondary school leaving the scheme by bus to go to the big school excited and terrified at the same time, surely this was normal for a 12-year-old? Those first days in class surrounded by feral looking kids with hand me down clothes, knee high Doctor Martin boots and shaved heads topped off with homemade tattooed knuckles making Frankie feel like a snob for the first time as he didn't join the queue to collect his free school meals ticket. He felt interrogated at times "Where are you fae?", "Whit team do you support?". He found it hard to front it but nobody seemed to notice he was putting a face on. Things changed for the better when he got his first fight under his belt. It involved him and a classmate who he actually liked, rolling about in the mud after exchanging blows for the first few minutes all because somebody challenged them to fight for their own entertainment. The classmate was a wee guy called Peter who Frankie had always gotten on with, there was no quarrel between the two but Peter like Frankie just didn't want to back down to the challenge made by the class bullies. The two were just too immature to see they were being manipulated. The result did Frankie no harm though and he walked a bit taller after that day. Although not a kid with any real ambition Frankie started school with the best of intention to stick in, do well in his exams and get a good job and make plenty of money. Truth is though he just lost interest. His mind was far more occupied with other things. He lived in the moment with no care for the future he was more concerned about adapting to his environment and thriving in the here and now. For a 12-year-old boy in 1980s Scotland that meant being hard, being funny or being cool. Fuck it Frankie wanted all three. He went from one extreme to another where he felt very much on the outside with butterflies in the stomach then to finding his feet and wanting to run the whole fuckin show.

Back to school after that first Christmas holiday he remembers seeing a few older lads coming onto the school bus head to toe in sportswear, Nike Windrunners, Sergio Tacchini tracksuit tops, white training shoes. He asked an older boy on the bus what they were wearing and he was told they were the casuals. It all looked so colourful and modern. Though he had no idea this look was related to football in anyway or how it would impact his life but he was hooked from day one. The big issue though was the cost. A Pringle lambswool jumper at £35.00 seemed so out of his reach but where there is a will there is a way and he got his first piece of branded clothing soon followed by a pair of Puma G Vilas to match. He thought how that was like a junkie taking his first hit and the young Frankie craved the elevated feeling these new clothes gave him. Through school fashion changed quickly and he had to keep up. Kappa Ski Jackets, Kickers Boots, Lyle and Scott jumpers, Ocean Pacific Sweatshirts, Benetton Rugby Tops, Nike Wimbledon trainers, Adidas gazelle, Lacoste Polo Shirts, Burberry Scarfs. He worked on paper rounds and milk vans to fund his addiction but as years progressed, he went to any lengths to get the desired item. Selling his old stuff, swapping two for one, snow dropping, shoplifting, taxing, smash and grab from motors there was little he wouldn't do to get what he wanted, no make that needed. He had little choice at times. He remembers a day when he was about seventeen, he tried on a pair of Timberland moccasins in a shop in Princess Square. He left the shop like Linford Christine leaving his old tatty trainers on the shop floor as the security guard chased him down Buchanan Street. Wearing the right clothes always seemed to have a dramatic effect on him and when he found that feeling he chased it, leaving any desire to be good and stick in firmly in childhood. Frankie was dipping his toe in the Casual thing at school but didn't start tagging along to the match until he was around fourteen where he met like mined souls who he felt an affinity with like never before in his wee scheme with the small-minded mentality and inter breeding. It was around then that he met Tommy at school. He approached Frankie in the playground dressed in a lemon lambswool jumper with a cool wedge haircut and asked Frankie about his trainers. The two had been inseparable ever since. Franke found a place of comfort within himself in the Casuals, an environment that may have intimidated others he felt he had found his tribe for the first time. It was during these Saturdays at the match he managed to get inside the pubs and he had rarely been out of them since.

Maybe the drink and adrenaline were familiar to him, a familiarity that comforted him. His early experience of drink was watching his parents and their friends in the house parties held throughout the scheme on a rolling basis where men with big sideburns and bigger guts drank McEwan's Lager from silver tankers and the women sipped Pils Lager and Carlsberg Special Brew as though it held some kind of elegance. Frankie and the rest of the kids were usually banished to one of the bedrooms while the adults drank and sang old songs. Normally happy affairs but there were times where his father finished the night early causing a fight making a right show of them. His father being the drunkest there leaving the young Frankie with a dull feeling he couldn't explain but he remembers walking home at a snail's pace with his head down just wanting to hide from the world. His mother and father would argue all the way home as his old man would try to justify his behavior. The next day it was business as usual. A pattern repeated by his old man throughout his time living at home as thought the embarrassment of the night before did not exist for him in his drunken stupor. Leaving the young Frankie to carry the burden which got heavier and heavier the older he got.

Frankie jumped into the shower as if attempting to break the thought pattern he was having. At times he could ruminate for hours on the one subject and never treasured childhood memories. Always the darkest of days he repeated on a loop in his mind trawling for worries to be taken care of or old scores to settle. There were times when he would end a relationship and still struggle to get his latest victim out of his mind but when together he would rarely think of them. He just couldn't switch his head off sometimes. He left the house dressed and, on a mission, but with no real plan of what to do as he had little business to take care of while still off work. He marched up the town on an exploration exercise, just a mooch about to see who was around while trying to avoid the cadgers, junkies and those who live in Ladbrokes. You were never short of company in this town when you had money in your pocket but that company could be choice to say the least. He was bored though and hated being at a loose end but had few interests these days apart from drinking and music. There were periods in his late teens where he was in the boxing gym three or four times a week, never a contender but fit as a fiddle and felt good for it. In his early twenties he lifted weights obsessively for a few years and cut down on the drinking and got his head together a wee bit but all these things had long since died out and he was left with the boozer.

He entered an old boozer he frequented in his dope

smoking days as the landlord turned a blind eye to them puffing as long as his till was full. It had a great Juke box back then and you could relax with your mates without any real concern of Police or bother. Frankie and Tommy had spent many hours in there when they were young, smoking and listening the Doors on loop as their teenage years were coming to an end. These days though with Cocaine the drug of choice for every wannabe bad boy in town the clientele had changed and he rarely went in there. It was early though still not quite noon and as good a place as any to start the day. Surprisingly there were a few of the younger lot from the mob in the pool room all full of the joys and on it still from the night before. He ordered a pint and joined them being met with an over friendly welcome telling him these lads were into the guts of a two-day session. He was welcomed into the company and joined the drinking pace finding his feet quickly and soon gaining a warm drink fueled glow as the cliched sound of 90s indie filled the room and every conversation was a look back at days gone by where the memory seemed like a Tarantino movie but Frankie lapped it up in the moment and the chat lifted his mood and took him out of his own head with the drink chilling his insides. He seemed to blink though and he was at the cross at closing time leaning against a traffic barrier talking to a guy he knew from school as the streets filled with drunk punters heading for home via taxi ranks and kebab shops. The quintessential British night out. An escape for the mundane where the masses forgot their worries and let their hair down at the end of the week some ending up with love and others sore faces. An attempt to find happiness in a place it never existed. Deep inside Frankie knew this though and the thrill of drinking had long since left him and he was now looking for something that just wasn't there for him. He craved a new scene to push him onto pastures green like when football was forgotten and the dawning of ecstasy came about. A new chapter began like an awakening for his generation shaking the hang ups off from the past like a mass spiritual awakening. He felt some new chapter for him was well over due like he was somehow cocooned but the new dawning never came leaving him on a mundane treadmill he didn't know how to get off.

He awoke the next day back at his flat with no recollection of getting home or little of the previous day's events with the familiar feeling of impending doom. The only face he could really remember after the boozer was Fleming a guy he had been going to the football with on and off since school days. It was rumored that Fleming had been dabbling in smack in recent months so had been blanked by many of the lads but Frankie had known Fleming a long time and knew his character well enough to know he was a decent enough guy. In saying that he wouldn't lend him any money or leave his wallet lying around unattended when Fleming was about. Knowing Fleming was alright still didn't make Frankie an idiot. Frankie had known a lot of guys who went down the smack route. Some were scumbags before smack but a few were decent guys who were destroyed by the drug in no time. One top boy in particular suffered an overdose which devastated the community and since then smack had been a bad word around here. Frankie had learnt certain life rules and stuck with them religiously, don't every lift your hands to a woman, never tell the Police anything and smack was a no no under any circumstances. This moral compass kept him from going down roads he didn't want to go down. Smack intrigued him if he was honest and at times, he felt a brown cuddle was just what he needed but he knew himself too well in that if he crossed that line there would be no going back for him.

Frankie stayed in the rest of the weekend on his own with the phone turned off and the light of the TV filling the room and he rarely moved apart from the odd trip to the toilet or kitchen where he lived off his usual diet of coffee, cigarettes and cornflakes. He would have stayed in longer but needed to get to the Doctor for a further sick line on the Monday morning and he got to the surgery with minutes to spare and was sitting in front of Dr Campbell before he had even time to think. When the Doc asked how he was feeling he was taken aback and felt a bit like a rabbit in the headlights as though he shouldn't need to answer these questions and the Doc should know how he felt. He almost answered "Fine" but remembered he NEEDED another sick line and medication so told the Doc he was "up and down" and felt his mood dip dramatically as the words left his mouth. He felt a relief when the Doc gave him another 4-week line and a prescription for 40mg Propranolol to be taken twice each day and fluoxetine 20mg to be taken once each day. Frankie left the surgery with the prescription in hand as though it a winning lottery ticket, he picked up the prescription, binning the Fluoxetine in the bin outside the chemist and kept the Propranolol which he would take in large doses as and when the anxiety crippled him.

His mind drifted back to a time before all this fuckin anxiety. A time he felt fearless with the arrogance of youth and excitement carrying him through his teens. Bravado he couldn't quite muster up now he was in his late 20s and wondered where had it all gone as there was a time, he cared for few. He remembered the day he first felt accepted by the mob on an awayday to Easter Road in the late 80s. Frankie and his group had hired a mini bus to travel to the match, stocked up with wine and high spirits all round they arrived in the nation's capital a good hour before kickoff. The bus parked on a few streets away from Easter Road and the group piled into a pub used by away fans every other Saturday. The pub was heaving with scarfers all half pished which was the usual for away games as the journey always involved drink. Frankie though only sixteen at the time was a seasoned pub drinker and felt the boozer his natural habitat at that early age. The pints flowed but soon it was time to go and the group left and headed down towards the stadium via the infamous Crawford Bridge or "The Bridge of Doom" as it was better known. Frankie felt a mass of excitement inside him as he knew the chance of an ambush by Hibs on the way down to the ground was highly likely as they were an organised mob who would always seem to appear from nowhere. One minute you could be facing a deserted street ahead and the next they would spring from pubs, closes, behind parked cars and every other possible hiding place only local knowledge could give. On a previous visit when Frankie had come by car a large group of CCS had chased him and his four comrades up Easter Road and

Frankie felt he had outrun them and was safe once again when a meat wagon approached very slowly, only for the driver to roll the window up and speed off when he seen what was happening leaving him to the mercy of Hibs mob. He learnt the deal in this part of Edinburgh early in his life which added to the day's excitement. No ambush today though as they crossed the bridge and down towards the old Dunbar End joining the queue to enter the ground with the away support filling the turnstile area with Hibs nowhere to be seen.

The group walked over the terracing towards the fenced area which separated the home and away fans on auto pilot as part of the day's entertainment would be a ninety-minute slagging match between the two mobs mocking each other's clobber or how shite their town was. As Frankie looked down the sloped terracing, he smiled to himself and the talk was how big a mob they had that day as here seemed to be maybe forty big boys already in place before they would even join them. The quality of their mob seemed to explain the no show by Hibs outside the ground. The pace towards their usual pitch was slowed though as they realized they did not recognize one face in the mob and that the mob they were about to join were Hibs who had the cheek to come in the away end. They quickly realised that their twelve seater mini bus would be no match for the superior numbers and were forced to blend in with the scarfers behind the away goal feeling well and truly defeated without even a blow being struck. The crowd settled down as the game got going but we kept our eye on the crowd and every move Hibs made as they sat on the terracing with an aura of superiority about them. An aura that would soon be crushed. Ten minutes into the game a trail of well-known faces began to appear from the turnstiles behind and word quickly got around that the older mob's bus had arrived a little late and the cavalry had arrived. Frankie and the others who had used the scarfers as camouflage began to move to the top of the terracing and welcome the cavalry quickly telling them of the liberty Hibs were taking coming in their end. Within a few minutes as the numbers swelled, instinctively the mob charged down the slope straight into the Hibs mob, punching and kicking as the two mobs clashed. Frankie was wearing a pair of red kicker boots and used the advantage of attacking from above by launching a massive kick straight into one of the Hibs mob who took the whole sole in the face as Frankie then wrestled the boy to the ground punching him as he went down as Frankie held him by the scarf and dragged him about like a wet tracksuit. The boy shrugged Frankie off eventually and ran for cover back to his mates but he left Frankie with a firm hold of the scarf. A camel Burberry checked scarf he still had to this day. Hibs were on the backfoot and the terrace was looking like a western with scuffles happening all over the fenced area as the Hibs boys in the home end chanted in support of their mates as they looked on helpless as they took a beating. Fairly quickly the old bill were on the terrace in mass and managed to split the two mobs up leaving Hibs with their tail firmly between their legs. Frankie never forgot the feeling of excitement that day as the Police led the mob out onto the street as the referee stopped the game and they ushered Hibs into their own end. They felt invincible and marched through Edinburgh along London Road towards Waverley singing the whole way feeling they could take the Zulu Army. The hired minibus was abandoned and they travelled as one as a mob safe in greater numbers. The train journey home was a party atmosphere and a feeling of unity was in the air as each told of the heroics, they had played in the days victory, some of which may have been true but you could never tell as in the heat of the moment there are no spectators only players. Tommy moaned all the way home as he had taken a penalty kick to the balls during the scuffle and the pain could still be seen on his face every time he moved much to the amusement of the lads. As the train pulled into Queen Street, they felt elevated as they walked along the platform towards the George Square exit as shoppers and daily commuters stood back wary of the mob of sixty or so youths. The adrenaline from Edinburgh had barely settled as they walked onto George Square to be met by a mob of Celtic Soccer Crew. A scruffy looking lot with last year's clobber on and scheme mentality. Certainly, no match for the mob approaching from Queen Street and they quickly realized it as they stood for what seemed like seconds and about turned and ran as they were chased through George Square. The unfortunate few brave enough to stand were punched and kicked to the deck being left to face their own humiliation and the betrayal by their mates to dampen their Saturday night. Frankie however had never felt so alive and sleep came very slowly that night as he lay in bed relaying the day's events over and over in his head as his body buzzed in anticipation for the next game. It only added to his excitement as the game had made the ten o'clock news that night and would be splattered all over the Sunday papers the next day. It was also the first time that Frankie knew they had been beaten 2-0!

4

Jam Tarts and Mushrooms

Sometimes life can be mundane, a repetition of previous days, experiencing the same over and over. Then there are times when life throws us a whirlwind bang out the blue. The Seventeen-year-old Frankie had no idea that his life was to change direction on that Saturday in 1989 as he entered the East Stand as he had done so many times before. He walked with his little crew towards the usual spot where they stood every other week taunting the away fans as they held the ace cards being the home team. It was a cold day with bubble coats being the fashion of the day with hair getting a little longer and jeans a little baggier. They looked as though they were attempting Everest rather than ninety minutes of football. Hearts at home and a fixture which stirred up little enthusiasm in him as he had never known their mob to come to them. They once had a fierce reputation as the Gorgie Aggro and terrorised many visiting fans to Tynecastle in the late 70s and early 80s but the CSF as the mob had become were a poor prodigy. Frankie expected a long ninety minutes watching a game he cared little for but maybe find his fun that weekend in a drunken haze later that night.

To his amazement as he approached the cage the away end was packed with lads shouting the usual put downs at them as their boys responded with equal bravado. Both sides of the fence hyper and in fits of giggles as they seemed to bounce around laughing and pointing the finger at one another. Frankie felt a disappointment though the talk was that Hearts were seventy or eighty handed and very few of their lads had made the effort to come out that day as they expected a no show. He was shocked at the appearance of Hearts but excited at the prospect of what would happen after the final whistle. Looking around the terracing among the scarfers, wannabes and lads Frankie counted about twenty of their lot in attendance. All good boys but just not the numbers to give Hearts any real challenge and they had won already by their turn out. This was an era way before the mobile phone and there would be no calling for back up and they would need to accept their lot.

Ten minutes before the final whistle their mob began making their way towards the exit and the group of twenty had swollen slightly as a few lads came out the woodwork as though realising that duty called as Hearts were no way going home unchallenged. The old bill would escort Hearts straight from the ground, quickest route to the train station which would mean taking them past the Police Station, Zanzi Bar and straight through the Shopping Precinct. The mob walked, almost jogged to get ahead of the Hearts mob taking the alternative route through the health centre only locals would know. They waited in anticipation at a gap in the tenement buildings before the underpass into the precinct. They arrived way before Hearts would get there. They were filled with excitement and anger. Anger that Hearts had the audacity to come to their town and flaunt it like they owned the shop, but worse anger at so many of their own boys who had failed to show leaving them on a suicide mission. There was talk among the lads about what to do when Hearts appeared but although this mob were small in numbers they were experienced and instinct would kick in as soon as Hearts came into sight. A long ten minutes passed as they watched a flow of scarfers in Maroon and White snake down the street until the first of a group appeared in the gap in the building without colours. As soon as they came into view the ambush was on and without any signal almost instinctively the mob sprinted towards them as though there was an understanding among them as they knew exactly what to do and when. The cat was firmly amongst the pigeons and Hearts scarpered unaware of the size of the mob they were up against being far less than half of what they had brought to town. There was roadworks being done on the street and the wee mob took full advantage hurling rubble and traffic cones straight at Hearts as they backed off instantly. Frankie looked right and one of the older lads was jogging down the street with a traffic cone in his hand like the Statue of Liberty before the cone came crashing down on a Hearts lads head. Frankie chose his victim who was about six feet from him as his sprint slowed to a jog and he swung a massive right hook mid run, hitting the lad on the side of the head causing him to stumble and fall and curl up hedgehog style as though he was about to be showered with further blows but almost instantly Frankie was wrestling with his mate who intervened to save the day. The guy was a tall skinny lad with shoulder length blonde hair who was wearing what can only be described as a shell suit. As the pair wrestled Frankie took the initiative to hold his opponent still and start throwing his right boot into his stomach and balls finally making him let go and back off with most of his mates. The adrenaline was pumping through Frankie's veins as carnage went on all round him with punches being thrown as well as road signs, bottles and bricks. The feeling of invincibility spread like wildfire and the guerrilla warfare style they had that day worked a treat as Hearts were well on the back foot. A few feet from him Frankie recognised the ginger hair of his mate McKelvie at waist height in a headlock who he though was being rag dolled by a Hearts boy and before he could help the one holding his mate in such a grip turned to stare directly at Frankie. Frankie froze for a second and his heart sank suddenly as he realised this stare was not from a designer clad youth looking for his Saturday fix but from one of Strathclyde's finest. The copper had removed his hat to help him blend into the crowd, it was the oldest trick in the book and Frankie hadn't noticed him. The big copper with McKelvie in a headlock in his left arm stretched out his right and grabbed Frankie by the scruff of the neck and began marching the two captives across the street to the awaiting meat wagon. McKelvie was flung into the half full mini bus style wagon and Frankie was second to be pushed in. There were few seats left in the meat wagon and by the time Robocop who had just nabbed two of them had gone fishing for more the wagon was full in no time and they were on their way to the Cop shop leaving Hearts safe to get the next train to old Edina and Frankie's weekend looking like counting tiles in the local nick.

The lads were booked in at the desk in no time and they

were banged up three to a cell. The first hour or so passed quickly as they laughed at the day's events and shared stories of who had done what and how they had well and truly done the Hearts mob. After that time began passing slowly and although this was Frankie's first arrest, the other two were old hat at this and it was debated whether they would be released that night or were in until Monday? Frankie shuddered at the thought at two days in here, having to shit in front of the other two and stress out without any cigarettes. He was reassured though that it was likely they would be released that night. The optimism of the early release was not wasted and only after a few hours the door was unlocked and one by one they were let out to attend court at a later date facing various charges ranging from Breach of the Peace to Mobbing and Rioting. Frankie didn't sweat the court charges as he knew many a lad who had been arrested umteen times without any real penalty. His mother and father however were a different story as his Fathers neurotic behaviour would guarantee some kind of episode when he returned home. His mother would either say fuck all and look at him in disgust or explode like dynamite dependant on her mood or how much Mogadon the Doctor had given her that week. Best to stay out as long as he could and he jumped on the first bus back up to the scheme knowing the arrest had solidified his place in the mob and further boosted his reputation just that wee bit more.

It was 9pm now and dark, Frankie strolled towards the bright light of the local off sales. The centre of the world for many in this concrete lego land. Before he reached the door of the shop he was greeted by a well-known local he knew only as Bud. Bud had almost legendary status in the scheme as was seen as a bit of a hippy type who had been too far off lands such as Amsterdam and Goa all in search of the best drugs known to man. He must have been at least ten years older than Frankie and was a tall man with longish hair who had abandoned the hippy look of his youth and now seemed very much the eccentric in his tweed jacket. Bud still uttered “man” at the end of most sentences though and to Frankie that meant a Hippy. Frankie had only previously exchanged a nod with Bud but tonight Bud asked the young Frankie where he was going on his own at this time on a Saturday night? Frankie only too keen to try to impress the almost mythical figure by telling him the tales of football violence and police stations and to his surprise Bud seemed to know quite a bit about the casual scene despite never having been part of it. In one of his previous adventures, he had teamed up with a crowd of Man Utd lads in Holland who were into football and working the concerts all over Europe. Unbeknown to Frankie the football lads from Manchester and Liverpool were heavily invested in drugs and crime in Holland and Bud had many a dealing with them.

Being at a loose end Bud invited the young Frankie to join him and his associate to drink in Buds flat assuring him that it was just a quiet one but he would be more than welcome. Frankie bought the appropriate carry out and joined the two older men back to the flat. Frankie was in awe when he entered the flat as it was decorated in paintings of Stonehenge, with Saris and Indian Rugs on the wall. A real mish mash of stuff gathered from a life well lived. The three made themselves comfortable by kicking off their shoes and removing their winter jackets and sat in a circle in the small tower block flat living room where they cracked open bottles and cans and began to relax a little though Frankie was still feeling the excitement from the day and now felt as though he was getting a peek into another world. A hippy world he knew little about. Bud produced a tray from under his armchair and began rolling a joint, sticking the skins together in a weird L shape Frankie had never seen before. Though Frankie pretended this was all a day at the office for him he was soaking wet behind the ears compared to these two. He asked Frankie to put some music on and he began digging through the vast pile of albums next to the turntable. Frankie has recently got into New Order and The Bunnymen and felt he was fairly clued up when it came to music but this collection was alien to him. Every Album cover had either a weird psychedelic picture or a picture of a medieval looking band. Frankie recognised the spectrum on Pink Floyds Dark Side of The Moon though at seventeen his knowledge of Floyd was minimal but he placed the record on the turntable and let the journey begin.

The trio chatted for a few hours devouring cheap wine and shitty Scottish lager as though they were feasting at a banquet and the mood relaxed with the weird music and dope. It was gone midnight and Bud returned from a toilet trip clutching a plastic carrier bag asking the young Frankie if he had ever tried mushrooms? Frankie had only ever heard magic mushroom stories and had taken acid a few times but never mushrooms. Bud held in the palm of his hand what looked to Frankie a bundle of dried straw, but when he looked closer, he seen the mushroom pinheads at the end of the stems and accepted the bundle into his own palm with the reassurance from Bud that he would be fine and that the amount he had given him was not a lot and he would have a nice mellow trip. No freaking out. Frankie crushed up the bundle as instructed and put the whole lot into his mouth. He chewed the vile tasting mushrooms quickly as he could and washed them down with a mouthful of wine which killed the putrid taste. He sat back in anticipation wondering what was going to happen but he was again assured that he would need to wait about half an hour before it kicked in. Another joint was rolled and beer was sipped in the smoke-filled room and Frankie felt content in the company as though he had some kind of connection with these guys. An atmosphere out with the casuals where he could let his guard down further. Pretty soon Frankie had a smile from ear to ear and found himself giggling slightly as the mushrooms took effect. This felt a bit more natural than the chemical experience of acid where you could almost feel the acid pulse in your veins. Soon though he has similar visions you got at the start of a trip where everything had a purple and green aura like the pictures in those old 3D comics. Not only that everything pulsed slightly as though breathing. Frankie felt happy. Ecstatic even and he sat giggling to himself watching his reality change before him with the weird sixties folk music Bud had selected playing in the background. Pretty soon Frankie had a full bladder and needed to pish. He entered the bathroom looking at himself in the mirror repeating over and over "this is fuckin mental!" as he held his cock firmly and pished into the toilet bowl. A wave of panic hit him like a ton of bricks as he was shaking it off. His cock totally disappeared and he had an empty palm in front of him. Frankie's mind raced as though his world had just ended. His most prized possession was gone! He sighed a sigh of relief as in the blink of an eye his cock reappeared exactly where it should be and he realised his mind was playing evil tricks on him. He buttoned up his jeans and went back into the living room laughing to himself while still feeling the relief that his cock was okay. As he sat back on the sofa any concept of time no longer existed and he didn't know if his toilet trip had been a few minutes, days or hours? He fixated his vision on the pair of desert boots Bud had left at the side of his armchair and laughed as the boots walked around the room as though the invisible man was break dancing in them. He laughed and laughed as the three went into their own little worlds staring aimlessly into space and timeless daydreams. His trip was broken as Bud asked him if he wanted to listen to some weird music? Although Frankie felt the previous Floyd and Incredible String Band, they had listened to was the weirdest music he had heard in his life mushrooms or not. He was intrigued and confirmed he was up for listening to anything. Nothing could have prepared him for The Gong Band and the spaced-out jazz he was about to experience which would take him to another level. This didn't even seem like music to him more some weird opera or satanic prayer. The next few hours seen him lying on the floor floating through the depths of his own mind as the music cloaked him in sound taking him to a place beyond thought. An inner world he didn't even know existed.

Eventually he must have passed into some kind of sleep as he came to the next morning still lying on the carpet in the recovery position feeling completely straight as though he had returned to earth again. He went to the toilet pished, wet his long hair flat again and and washed his face. He returned to the living room to meet the other two smoking dope again and smiling asking him how he was? Frankie's face said it all with the smile he presented them with but he couldn't find the words to tell them what he had experienced. They knew though and there was now a bond between them. Frankie refused any more hash as it was only 8am an he was yet to reach the dizzy heights of the three-day bender so familiar to his older comrades and he made his excuse and left.

The flat he just left was to become a like a second home to him over the next period of his life. A place where he could retreat to and Bud became like some kind of kindred spirit. They spent many a night debating life's complexity in there. Sometimes over tea and biscuits and others enough drink to keep the two happy for days. Always smoke and music. Bud helped mentor Frankie through the latter part of his teenage years and the issues he faced with the opposite sex. Bud used his life experience to Frankie's advantage. They talked and talked and Bud introduced him to Dylan, John Martyn, Neil Young, The Doors, Roy Harper, Donovan and various other poets and wizards. Frankie felt a connection to Bud like he had never before, a friend for life he thought. However, it wasn't to be. Bud lived life by his own philosophies and was just too sensitive for this world as he never saw his fortieth birthday. His love for excess would be his downfall and his demise left a mark on Frankie that would never fully heal.

That first meeting changed Frankie though, it made him re-evaluate who he was. The casual scene which he had been so obsessed with had suddenly been side stepped in one day as he was introduced to a world of soul searching and weird music. A world of altered states of consciousness and individuality. Which path would he choose now? Had Frankie just found himself a little? Only time would tell and the life experience Bud had which Frankie valued so would need to be lived not taught to him. Only time would tell what Frankie's story would look like.

5

For the wings of a dove

The experience on the mushrooms had changed the young Frankie's priorities. It even made the constant grief from his Parents all worth it and he didn't even know about the pending court case yet. He would hopefully be out of the house soon when he got a decent job as the Youth Training Scheme, he had started wasn't even enough money to get him through the weekend or buy decent clobber. Luckily for Frankie his mate Deano had a cracking scam right now where he was buying credit cards from a postman he knew. The Postie would know which envelopes contained the plastic cards and would keep one or two aside selling them onto Deano who would sign the cardholders name in his hand writing. Deano would then go into the toon suited and booted and speak in a Spam valley accent buy a few hundred quid's worth of clobber in various stores throughout the toon and sell the stuff on for a fraction of the price. You could even order what you wanted on his next escapade and it would be dropped off the following week. It kept Frankie looking the part though he had pennies in his pocket most days. He felt he was a man now he was working and could do what he wanted, so fuck his Mum and Dad. When he moved out he could forget all about his arsehole parents and the madness he called a home. He still went to the match on a Saturday but there were fewer and fewer lads turning up each week and only the hardcore remained. Some had drifted away altogether. More lads were getting into music in a bigger way, some choosing the indie bands like the charlatans but most getting into House Music. Some were even bedroom DJs. Clothes were getting baggier for all but more prominently the fighting was fading out. As for Frankie he was becoming obsessed with dope. Since that night in Buds, Frankie and his little crew would meet most nights and smoke as much as they could afford. They were too young to have a flat so they were stuck standing in the woods smoking joint after joint. It became a badge of honour if you could roll the perfect joint and how much you knew about Hash. Soft black, Rocky, Lebanese, Soap Bar even Diesel which they doubted was even Hash. They began listening to all sorts of music. Frankie hated this new electronic House Music most were into he preferred guitar bands and got into Bod Dylan and The Doors. Some lads once dressed head to toe in labels even began wearing Pink Floyd t-shirts. The culture was changing overnight and many were telling tales about local raves they had been at and the mind-blowing effects of the ecstasy tablets they had been taking. Frankie felt this was a lot of shite and hated the music and felt DJ's were merely playing records and saw no reason why they were being help up like superstars.

Slam in The Park was happening in Strathclyde Park and few lads from his work were talking about it and Frankie was beginning to feel like he was the last guy on earth not to have been to a Rave of any kind so reluctantly agreed to tag along even although he had decided it just wasn't his scene.

Tommy and the others were now fully fledged ravers and had shoulder length hair and were wearing bright trainers and long-sleeved Italian football shirts when they met at the cross that night. Tommy loved the whole dance music thing and had bored Frankie with it for months as he still listened to Dylan. Tommy was buzzing like an old fridge as they walked to the park telling Frankie how amazing this was going to be. Frankie was yet to be convinced of the whole thing and felt like this would be a one off for him. They stood in the park for a bit drinking wine and smoking joints before entering the huge marquee which was jam packed and the music pounded out beats shaking the place up. Frankie had not really danced since he was into Ska when he was really young but he bounced about a bit feeling self-conscious even although he had a fair amount to drink before they entered the tent and the joints were being passed around constantly. He still carried an uneasy feeling as though he was being watched making him feel clumsy and stiff as he tried to dance. He just tried to go with the flow copying the moves of those around him. Tommy was encouraged him to half and E with him and assured him he would love it. Tommy's enthusiasm was infectious and he quickly convinced Frankie it was the right thing to do. At this point he felt like a total square for not doing it too and Frankie felt he knew the script with his daily dope smoking and his mushroom trip so agreed even although half this wee white tablet would cost him a tenner. Tommy disappeared into the crowd and came back ten minutes later showing Frankie the white tablet in the palm of his hand telling him it was a Dove and they were the best. Tommy broke the tablet in half using his nails and handed Frankie his half which they both quickly swallowed washing it down with the lager from the cardboard pints they had been drinking. Frankie felt a little guilty as he swore, he would never take drugs when he was younger but had taken to Hash like a duck to water but again swore, he would do no more than smoke dope yet here he was breaking his own rules again by taking yet another tablet. Although he was curious about the feeling ecstasy gave you and wanted to know for himself but it was almost like starting drinking when he was a boy he just really wanted to fit in and at times he just didn't know his own mind. The group continued to dance and talk a bit and Frankie just looked around him as there were so many girls wearing next to nothing and so many guys with eyes half closed and jaws sticking out. It was alien to him. Another world he had yet to discover.

Around half an hour later (Its always half an hour) he felt like he could feel something flowing through his veins but he couldn't really be sure or describe it. There had been little talk under the pounding music and had spent the time dancing about mostly. Tommy put his arm around Frankie's shoulder and shouted in his ear, can you feel it yet? As the words left Tommy's lips a Tsunami of happiness rushed through Frankie's body from the tips of his toes to the top of his head. He felt it so powerful he was going to have to sit down. He knew by the look on Tommy's face he was feeling it too. Tommy seen Frankie was struggling a bit and told him to keep dancing or he would gouch and the two smiled at each other and bounced up and down a bit with

Frankie thinking no way could this be real. The feeling was indescribable and he now knew how these wee tablets were called ecstasy. Within a short period, the rush seemed to become part of him and he felt comfortable with it as if he was at home. All inhibitions vanished and he felt at one with the world. Time slowed down and the music uplifted him, he started to see the vibe with this house music. It was happy, positive. It spoke of unity and love. Frankie couldn't help but go with the flow and he spent the whole night dancing and talking to total strangers. Hugging everyone he met. He no longer felt anyone was looking at him and he wanted to speak to everyone, know them, love them, find out everything about them, their hopes dreams, fears. The sweat drenched his body and the Armani t-shirt he had recently got from Deano who had kindly fleeced the newly opened Emporio Armani shop is Glasgow was like a wet rag with the neck line half way down his chest. He really didn't care. Vanity was out the window. For a guy who had spent his youth watching out for other mobs, guys from other areas, constant mayhem in the house he felt he could finally be free of constantly being on high alert. This was euphoria, he felt equal to all and he didn't want the night to end. When the lights came on in the big tent and the music finally stopped, he felt like he had the best night of his life and he would remember it forever. The crowd slowly made their way out onto the concrete area at the side of the loch and stood about talking for a while wondering where they were going to keep the vibe going. Nobody wanted this night to end. Some would drive home, others stay in the park for hours. Frankie and his mates had met a crowd from the east end who had been into the scene for a while and knew the routine of the two-day party. They were invited to join them back at a flat in Easterhouse which was only a ten-minute drive from the park. The Glasgow crowd had a transit van they could pile into and keep the party going back at their flat. As Frankie walked to the van, he looked at his shoes and they had a white tide mark around them as though he had been walking in snow but it was just sweat constantly pouring off him with the body heat and the E. He didn't give a fuck though. He felt like he had known the crowd from the east end all his life and there was a connection between them all. Before they piled into the flat, they stopped at their local shop and stocked up on drink, cigarettes and Rizla and entered the block of flats where some continued to dance in the smoke-filled living room. Frankie found himself sitting at the kitchen table with a group of seasoned ravers who he talked and talked with about anything and everything. The ecstasy was wearing off now but the hash kept the vibe mellow and he would have bared his soul to this lot and they did the same with him. They talked about their love for music, songs that touched them, places they had been to or wanted to go to. Ibiza, Amsterdam, Berlin, Goa. There was such a big world to explore out there and Frankie wanted it all. He didn't care that he was matted with sweat or how he looked. He felt equal. He felt close to the dreadlocked girl next to him as they talked about what they wanted to do with their lives but this was not a sexual vibe more just two folk connecting. The horn would hit him later when he was home alone and he would feel a little regret at not making a move on one of the girls he was surrounded with but the ecstasy just didn't give him that kind of urge. They promised to meet the Glasgow crowd the following weekend as they left the flat later that afternoon. As he walked down the stairs of the block of flats it dawned on him that the place, they had ended up in was an out and out shithole and they were taking their lives in their hands even being here. They had heard of the reputation Easterhouse had but never ventured off the motorway into the scheme before and it was a real no go zone unless you were a local but the ecstasy had banished any fear or caution on the way in. Now it was time to get the fuck out and they laughed at each other as they headed out the flats into the waiting taxi.

Frankie felt free and elated as he later lay in bed, as though he had been given a peek into a secret world that only the chosen few knew. He thought about his parents and the cunts in work and how their lives seemed so dull and boring to him. He wasn't even asleep from the rave yet and he was planning next weekend. The problem with the weekend being so brilliant is that during the week now became so dull and mundane. He just couldn't be arsed with the small talk in work or the constant bullshit from his Parents. He wanted to live a life where he could be free. Free of the life that his parents had lived and be an individual doing what made him buzz. He just wanted to be happy and somehow loosen this vice he felt tighten around him at times.

Frankie still went to the match but even he was now going less and less as his weekends were just one long party not like in the drinking days where he went home on Friday night and got up again on Saturday to start again. The weekend just never ended. He lost a ton of weight only eating 5 days a week and the constant dancing. He really was living the dream and the fun went on forever. His little crew travelled all over the country to find Raves. Initially there were small local ones in The Hatonrigg Hotel in nearby Bellshill but eventually it was Ayr, Saltcoats, Dunfermline, Stirling and anywhere they could get to. They made loads of friends from all over and the desire to fight at football just left him. He worried sometimes at the damage he was doing to his brain with all the pills and powder but mostly the fun he was having outweighed any fear quickly and he felt fuck it if I die young this is worth it. It felt like he and Tommy had become more like Brothers than friends.

Some places were full of cheezy quavers as they were known with their bandannas and dungarees, some even held glow sticks and blew whistles. Others were full of football lads still dressed head to toe in the terrace attire of the day in Ralph Lauren and Timberland footwear. Initially he was on edge when he recognised a few old faces he had gone toe to toe with in the past but mostly the pills took away any anxiety and there was little trouble and if there was it was usually relating to drugs and who was selling what.

His eutopia was to end though and one night when he was leaving Ayr Pavilion, he waited on a mini bus near the sea front and he felt his heart was going to burst out his chest and he struggled to get breath. He thought for a minute that he was going to pass out and had to sit down on the pavement with a few passing ravers asking if he was okay. Frankie was bewildered and confused but the feeling soon passed and he found his feet again but the episode shook him up and he began worrying more about his health. Did he have some king of panic attack that night or was the weekend drug taking finally catching up on him? Who knows, but all he knew was that he was starting to feel less euphoric and care free and a knot appeared in his stomach from then on, a knot that would haunt him from that day on.

The relationship he had with his father was deteriorating as he didn't approve of him disappearing all weekend and continued to try to control his every action, it was hard work continually lying to him to avoid criticism but nothing really worked. His Father was the type of man if you gave him the sun it would be the wrong colour and he just seemed to get off on hassling him constantly. This added to his hyper sensitive state. That and the fact he was constantly carrying some kind of drug and avoiding detection from family or the Police also made him feel he was living in a few different worlds. One where he was constantly in party mode with the sole purpose of being alive was to reach an altered state and another where he was hassled by his drunken Father or had to mix with the straight pegs in work who he also had to lie to when they asked what he was doing at the weekend. He fretted if any of these worlds would cross and if he was with a workmate at lunchtime and bumped into someone from the weekend, he would feel uneasy as though the roles he was playing would clash and he would be found out somehow.

With his Twenty-first birthday looming and his head feeling like a washing machine most of the time he had no choice but to make some changes to his life. This decision didn't come quickly or easily but only after months of not sleeping, thinking too much, impending doom following him around and a knot in his stomach he was to fight against for years to come and a feeling like jaggy nettles were under his skin rarely leaving him. This angered Frankie at times as he seen others around him who had been on the rave scene way before him and had partied harder than he had and were still smiling from ear to ear and loving the life, while he felt like screaming inside at times. The self-conscious thoughts of his secondary school days were consuming him again and he was struggling with his confidence. The bravado he once had when entrenched in the casual scene seemed to have dulled in him a little and he began feeling unsure of himself at times and he felt he needed to dig himself out of the hole he was in. He looked around at some guys he went through school with. Some previously nobodies who had become bodybuilders, hitting the gym most days and living a far healthier lifestyle than Frankie which had seemed to pay off for them as they were now confident, self-assured even. Some doing well in work with decent girlfriends and life falling into place. He thought he could hit the gym and burn off this prickly feeling of anxiety he carried under his skin, sort his head out a bit. Maybe he could take up boxing again or do some martial arts and get fighting fit, literally. He seen some who were car obsessed and every penny went on the latest gadget for their souped-up Vauxhall Nova or Ford Escort. Truth is though he just couldn't muster up any enthusiasm like these guys could and didn't feel the passion they had and he honestly felt most of them wankers. It was still important to Frankie to wearing the right clothes and be part of something but he was beginning to feel he didn't fit any longer and needed to shed his skin somehow. He just didn't want to fade into insignificance.

That next weekend he stayed in. This was never heard of and time passed slowly for him in front of the portable TV in his bedroom. At times he felt relieved that he had taken some action to change things then he would then get a wave of sadness and felt like crying into his pillow. Like always though he kept the face on and fronted it to the world while his stomach was in knots. He slept half the weekend as his body was mind were exhausted. Exhausted from the years of avoiding sleep and thinking too much when he was awake. He felt safe when he was on his own and was beginning to feel raw when he had to face the world straight. He hadn't smoked dope or drank all weekend. This was a milestone for him as he hadn't done this in years. The next few weeks he spent going to work and staying in. While at work he felt alright most of the time but his palms sweated constantly and his guts churned. He was like a live wire at times and felt that he was under attack when the banter flowed at work even though he managed to keep a face on it and join in giving the impression he was made of Teflon.

The boredom got the better of him and he felt determined to lose the buzzing anxiety which never quite disappeared and a few weeks into his new quiet life he dug out his old wraps and gloves and took himself back to the boxing gym. He loved the atmosphere in there. The smell of sweat, blood on the ring and bags wrapped with duct tape. The beat of the lads skipping and hammering bags was music to his ears and he felt at home in there. The gym attracted a few characters who had faces of lives lived on the other side of the track but boxing had saved them. The discipline in the room and the mutual respect ensured this was a safe place even although this would be intimidating to some. Frankie knew all was well within these four walls. The old guy who ran the gym knew the score only too well and weeded out any wanna be hardmen quickly or the sport made men of them. Frankie could use this place to help him heal a little and get well. He went as often as he could and loved the sound of the leather skipping ropes flying past his ears as he skipped round after round before pounding bag after bag. It was hypnotic to him almost like the house music he had once hated. He even got in the ring within a few months as his confidence built up and he felt the self-doubt leaving his body with the beads of sweat that poured off him every time he trained. As he showered after each session, he would feel free again, free of his own head and free of the knot in his stomach.

Frankie enjoyed feeling fit. He was lean and felt good. The boxing filled his time and gave his life some purpose. He felt alone though, those 48 hours between leaving work Friday and Sunday dinner time he felt like the only guy his age who stayed in. Staying in and avoiding life. A life he once lived to the fullest but here was at only twenty-one years of age scared. Scared of the places he could go in his mind if he kept living the life he lived. Was he destined to a life of doom and gloom and diet coke for the next forty years? Surely not.

He felt sure he was finished with the drugs as he knew he was playing Russian roulette with his mind if he kept it up. A few beers on a Friday couldn't hurt though, could it?

6

Go square go

Fight! Fight! Fight! Fight! Is chanted in unison like some jungle tribe taking part in a ceremony they are all too familiar with. This is a different tribe though. None bigger than five foot tall. Wee lassies in pigtails and duffle coats and wee boys with leather satchels slung over their shoulders like a cheap Harry Potter remake set in Lanarkshire.

Frankie views the scene around him from the solid grey concrete he lies on arms stretched out like a zombie holding a wee boy by the throat as the boy's fists windmill into Frankie like a Tasmanian Devil. Frankie throws the boy aside like a wet tracksuit and gets back onto his feet before he is swallowed by the crowd of school weans who are moving in and out like waves making the ring, he has found himself in get bigger the smaller as the chant of Fight! Fight! Keeps on ringing in his ears.

Just as Frankie finds solid footing the Tasmanian Devil of a schoolboy charges him again. Fists up and chin down with two piercing eyes focused firmly on Frankie as the two lock arms as like Stags locking horns. Frankie's nearly two foot taller than the boy and should easily be able to over power him but its like he just can't muster up the strength and the wee boy has super powers. Frankie manages to toss him aside and boot him as he hits the deck for the umpteenth time but like the previous times the boy refuses to stay down and no matter how many blows Frankie lands, he seems to remain unscathed and springs back on his feet almost instantly ready to go again.

Frankie's heart is nearly beating out of his chest and his eyes scan the crowd for a saviour to come and save the day, it seems like he has been fighting forever and no matter what his pint-sized opponent won't stay down. The panic rising in him isn't through fear of this opponent. Every round Frankie wins hands down. The Fear is not knowing when this will be over?

Every punch, every kick Frankie lands is punishing the boy. Doing what it is supposed to do. Seconds later though its like the previous blows never mattered and the boy is right in front of Frankie again. Eager to be set free to maul Frankie like a tormented pit bull.

The crowd love every minute and could watch the two wrestle and gauge at each other all day as Frankie continues to exchange blow after blow with the boy without a face. The boy Frankie knows only too well. He has been fighting him for years.

The bell goes as always and Frankie reaches his right hand out of the duvet and hits the stop button on his 7.30am alarm. His mind and body are filled with the comfort of relief that it was only a dream. A dream Frankie has been having for years and like every other time he is grateful to be wakened back to reality. The reality of a bed saturated in sweat and a grown man wondering why he keeps fighting wee boys in his dreams and why this dream scares him shitless.

Frankie puts a Benson between his dry pursed lips and flicks the wheel on his clipper sending smoke deep into his lungs as his thoughts waken to reality.

7

Blood on the tracks

Last game of the season and it was Rangers at home. A sea of red white and blue would soon descend on the whole town with the prospect of them winning the league and pipping their arch rivals Celtic to the post on the last game. It would be a memorable one whatever the result and we were safe from relegation and had nothing to lose except our pride.

Frankie felt a mix of excitement at the unknown of what the day ahead would bring but he was also a little bit wary as Rangers were blade merchants and he had seen first-hand how they cut people with the same ease as he threw punches. He quickly realised that smoking a joint with breakfast may not be the best idea to put him in the frame of mind he needed for the day ahead. He stubbed the roach out in the ashtray as he realised, he was already thinking too much and needed to shake it off and get in the right groove. There was no room for self-doubt today of all days.

He quickly brushed his teeth and pushed back his long damp hair before tying the laces of his Travel Fox trainers. He headed out of his flat, locked the door and tried to get a swagger on as he headed up to the towers. Underneath the arrogant exterior he tried to project he felt a niggling in his stomach as his brain raced as he scowered the streets as he walked. He knew he needed drink to chill him out a wee bit. As much as the anxiety niggled at him a bigger part of him wanted to boot the ICF right back to Glasgow and show them they couldn't come here and take the piss with their inbred fans singing shite about King Billy and fucking the Pope. These were weird times he thought. Everyone growing their hair and smoking dope like the 60s again but head to toe in designer clothes and fighting like fuck on a Saturday. Sometimes he struggled to switch from the peace and love vibe to all guns blazing over the course of 24 hours. Nobody else seemed to give a fuck though so he just carried on regardless.

He approached the foot of the tower which held the local carry out shop and saw there was a fair few lad already congregated there drinking wine and cans and carrying on among themselves. Spirits were high with the day ahead pending. The sun was splitting the trees and he was welcomed with open arms by all as he was a well-known face but had little time for pleasantries and nodded through the lads and straight into the shop. He cracked his wine before he was even handed his change and had the neck out of it before he was back out of the shop. He had barely consumed enough to give him a glow but mentally he felt better immediately. Holding the bottle like a comfort blanket knowing that the contents would alter how he felt and shake off this uneasy feeling. The empty bottle might come in handy too he thought. He joined the lads outside the shop and asked what the script was for the day ahead? Frankie was worried that the rave scene had stolen so many good boys from the football that the mob was dwindling a bit. They were left with a weird mix of the real hard core old heads and a bunch of new kids on the block who had no experience. In the heat of the moment the older lads would lead the way and the adrenaline should push the others to follow suit. The wee mob grew and grew and there were now about forty of them which was enough to go ahead with anyone but they still needed more boys. Forty was not quite enough for Rangers who would bring a big mob for last game of the season. Enough to have a good go if they bumped into them before everybody was out though. There was a weird atmosphere today. More serious somehow than the normal feel at the football where despite the violence was all seen as a bit of a laugh. Today they meant business though. Rangers were arrogant and acted like they ran the show. Not today though, they would be met will full resistance no matter what the odds.

As the alcohol took effect anticipation disappeared as Frankie felt more in the moment his head had slowed down a bit. Any concerns were gone. No thoughts of getting slashed, arrested or worse. Just right here and now. The mob walked from the cover of the tower block and headed to the Civic Centre in the middle of the town a good place to hide and keep an eye out from all angles. As they entered the carpark of the big brutalist building, they saw about twenty lads hanging about in the close area. Twenty lads who were all focussed on the mob approaching and hackles were getting up until they became into clear view. Friendly faces. The two mobs amalgamated with smiles and hugs exchanged between the boys. The numbers swelling had caused another surge in confidence as they spoke of what way the ICF would pass. It seemed more likely they would pass via the precinct with hopefully few coppers in toe. A few shorties were sent to see what was what from both roads passing the Civic. One of which Rangers would have to take to reach the ground for kick off. The mob stayed put in the close area eagerly awaiting the mayhem they would create in the next half hour. The anticipation was building and becoming unbearable. Frankie had witnessed on several occasions where fights would break out between the boys if they had nobody to release this energy on. In house fighting was uncommon but it did happen if there was a no show from the opposition and the lads were wound up. All generally forgotten about the next day.

Two shorties suddenly appeared at the top of the stairs as though a bomb had gone off. "They're coming!! "They're coming!!". Adrenaline kicked in and almost instantly the lads headed up the stairs in mass shouting and egging each other on to get into the Rangers mob. Perfect timing as Rangers were only a stone's throw away as the ambush snaked out onto the street and appeared in front of them to the surprise of Rangers and the few Police that were around them in a pathetic escort. Bottles and bricks were rained down on Rangers and they responded instantly in the way only an experienced mob would and charged forward at the first break in the missiles. The two mobs clashed initially with just the dozen or so at the front exchanging firm blows but then the two mobs almost amalgamated with fist and boot flying. The ICF were on the back foot with the surprise attack and they backed off slightly but in no time at all they regrouped with a few of their older lads at the front organising the counter attack they charged forward in full force and the two mobs clashed again with bodies dropping like flies on the concrete pavements as the chaos ensued.

Frankie was in fairly near the front. He knew the best tactic was always to get in first and hit hard and get back out before the Police started grabbing folk. Half the time it was stragglers who got lifted to make them look as if they were doing their job and keep their stats up. He exchanged punches and kicks with a Rangers lad who had a leather baseball cap on like something out of New Jack City. The two rained blows on each other then both took a few steps back and shared a knowing look that said "Fair Play Mate" as they both retreated back to avoid the growing number of florescent jackets and truncheons that were mixing with the casuals.

By now the Police were doing their best to keep the two mobs apart and there were those so engrossed in the fighting that they were being grabbed and dragged to the awaiting meat waggons that had arrived on the scene. It was time to get the fuck out of there and try and keep your freedom.

Frankie ran back down the stairs with most of his mates around him and they jogged back through the civic and headed towards the ground slowing the pace as they mingled with the football crowd and tried to act inconspicuous. The adrenaline was pumping though and there were smiles all around with tales being told of what each had contributed to the ambush and who had been lifted. It had been a decent dash and Rangers had held their own but it felt like a victory in the sense that it was their town and they had provided the expected welcoming committee and their reputation was firmly intact. This was all before kick-off and there was still after the game to look forward to.

The game dragged on for Frankie. He hated football. He never really understood the male obsession with 22 guys booting a ball about a park. It had always bored him from childhood and his disinterest in the game had made him feel alienated from the majority at school who played it constantly and talked about it obsessively. It meant nothing to him. He was drawn to the terraces like a working class fashion catwalk of trainers and the best clothes. This led him to becoming steeped in the casuals which gave him a sense of belonging he had been void of before. He felt part of something. Something to be proud of. Something to defend. Something that belonged to them and only them. He gained some notoriety being a casual which elevated his self-esteem. It was tailor made for him. Like the mods of the 60s this was their thing and only theirs. Something the majority of the population knew little of and those who did know did not understand it.

He spent most of the game talking to an old school mate Broony who had almost made it as a professional boxer but his love of drink had distracted him from the ring and his ticket out of the scheme. He was firmly in the cycle of benders, getting off it, getting fit, back on the drink and forgetting about the gym and round and round he would go. Soon the gym and the ring would be a story to tell in the pub of who he used to be. Like so many Scottish men trapped by the bottle. Broony was one of those guys who had a humility about him that

Frankie admired. Broony never acted hard or bullied anyone. He just knew what he could do and so did everybody else. He had nothing to prove. All round good guy who was liked by all. Broony would always ask how you were? How the family were? And seemed genuinely interested. A guy Frankie could talk to about anything but he was also glad he was not in his close circle as he felt if he got to know him too well he would suddenly become human like everyone else and Frankie wanted his time with Broony to remain uplifting. He didn't want the shine to dim in any way.

The game was dragging on with the hatred being chanted by both sets of fans now. One each and a fairly eventful game with fifteen minutes to go. The result meant nothing to them and they would finish mid table as they always did. Far more important for Rangers who were always in a two-horse race chasing the title. Five or six of them decided to head to the pub, Frankie was surprised they lasted that long as the lure of drink normally won most Saturdays with some travelling home and away and rarely seeing a ball being kicked. The streets around the ground were far from deserted although the game was still in play many left early to beat the traffic when the Old Firm were in town. The group were in good spirits and the day had been a good one so far but it was far from over. On auto pilot they crossed the road to the grey concrete of the Civic once more to access the pub via the back door like they usually did after the game. Defences were down and the comradery of their local was calling. As they neared the back steps with the first couple climbing down the steps Broony shout wait! Who the fuck is that? As about twenty lads appeared from the right heading straight towards them with a bit of a jog picking up. They must have been hiding in the shadows before they knew they were there. Suddenly Frankie was punched from the side out of eye line just as he was at the top of the stairs. The blow was like a sledge hammer hitting him and not just because he was sucker punched but there was weight behind it and he lost his footing instantly and tumbled straight down the concrete stairs taking stones off in skin as he rolled down the concrete. Broony was throwing punches instantly and the others scrambled up the stairs and charged into the attacking mob who outnumbered them four to one. Frankie lay at the bottom of the stairs dazed but knew he had to get back on his feet. He stumbled to get up and fell back on his arse with his head still spinning a bit then the world came back into focus and he pushed himself back up onto his feet his legs feeling solid once more. He looked around frantically for something he could use as a weapon before he ran back up the stairs. The area at the side of the pub was littered with empty silver beer barrels and bright coloured crates with piles of empty bottles. Frankie ran back and grabbed two empty Budweiser bottles and ran back up the stairs which were now cleared as the fighting was now taking place all over the carpark with his mates taking on two at a time and being booted about by their attackers. He held a bud bottle in each hand by the neck and lifted his right arm in the air and launched one of the bottles at two of the Rangers mob who were lost in the fight. The bottle spun threw the air and hit one of them on the shoulder making little impact but was enough to make them back off for a minute and take stock of where the flying bottles were coming from. Frankie put the remaining bottle in his right hand and ran towards a chubby Rangers lad who was wearing one of those Rule Britannia type Hackett Polos. As he ran towards him, he raised the bottle above his head and as he neared the fat boy he swung the bottle down as hard as he could keeping a firm grip of the neck of the bottle. The bottle smashed on impact leaving Frankie with only a few inches of the neck still in his grip. The fat boy was now crouched over holding his shaved head and screaming. Breaking the bottle on his thick skull must have been like a blow from a baseball bat and the broken glass had cut him instantly as the blood was spewing between his fingers and dripping onto the concrete below. Frankie's eyes widened as he viewed the devastation in front of him. Devastation he had caused. He instantly regretted his actions and the adrenaline leaving his body was now taken over by fear. What the fuck had he done? Time began to slow to a standstill and Frankie looked at the neck of the bottle in his right hand. He dropped it as soon as he realised it was still in his grip and began walking slowly backwards. The sudden bottle attack had made both sides regroup slightly and take in their surroundings, the game must have ended and the streets around them were filling up with scarfers. The two groups merely walked in different directions with a few of the Rangers lads comforting their cut mate who looked as though he was wondering what the fuck had just happened as his face was covered in blood. Rangers had dealt out a good beating with their superior numbers but the bottle had evened up the score a wee bit. Fat boy looked gutted as his mates led him away soaked in blood as both sets of lads made themselves scarce.

Frankie and the others headed off past the pub and took a right towards Glencairn Tower where Tommy had a flat. They walked as slow as they could trying to act normal with the adrenaline pumping through their veins they looked far from normal. They stuck out from the rest of the football fans around the streets like you could almost see their vibration. Safely inside Tommy's flat Frankie could relax a bit. The others were laughing and joking about what had just happened exchanging war stories and showing off bruises with pride. They done well considering the odds. Frankie was glad he had escaped what could have been a major kicking and he had thought on his feet but he didn't feel good about what he had done to that boys face. No matter how much he hated Rangers and they knew the score he didn't want to cut anybody. He was already getting worried thoughts about repercussions, Police looking for him, that bottle neck he dropped would be covered in his finger prints he thought. Would he do jail for this? Could he handle the Bar-L?

He downed the can that Tommy had handed him in an attempt to slow his head down a wee bit and join in the comradery they shared. They had stuck together and all were in good spirits despite the bruises and grazes they displayed. Pride was intact. The bond between them was strong but Frankie felt as though if the shit hit the fan over this he would be the one taking the fall. Why did everybody else in this world seem to not give a fuck but he worried about everything? His head kept him awake at night with a constant stream of what ifs and he went between worried to being almost aloof with arrogance and confidence at times. He rarely found the middle ground he so desired. Tommy smiled at Frankie as if to provide some reassurance as Tommy knew Frankie only too well and would know he was worried. Tommy knew who the real Frankie was.

Maybe his chaotic upbringing had shaped him more than he thought. Maybe his crazy father had rubbed off on him and he just couldn't shake him off. His constant criticisms and how he continually tried to control him had made him feel bad about himself and guilty when there was no guilt at his door. He felt he had a good view of the world and liked most other folk but he was damaged somehow by him. His father's darkness had seemed to seep into his bones and affect him. Like a Siamese twin he dragged about with him getting heavier and heavier. He had a sense of impending doom hanging over him, like his world was going to end soon if things were going well and if there was trouble to handle, he catastrophized it and put himself in the worst possible outcome. Anything he had achieved in life he had to fight through his own negativity and self-doubt to get there. Life was like wading through treacle at times while everyone around him seemed to float past with ease.

After the few cans Tommy had to offer ran out the pub was calling them. The tap had been open and it wouldn't be closed until tomorrow at least. The wee group entered the crowded pub and while the drinks were ordered Frankie was crowded by some of the other lads interrogating them on today's events. He suddenly lost any guilt and retold the tale replaying the event over with big hand gestures and smiles. He didn't give a fuck anymore and he seemed to be okay with things once more. They were elevated in the eyes of their friends for a night. Heroes almost. Frankie playing the part of the hardman who didn't give a fuck. Inside he felt like a fraud. He knew it was only half true. The drink was dulling his fears but inside he could feel the worry growing. How badly had he cut the fat boy? Had he disfigured this guy for life? Sure there was more than enough justification but it still didn't sit well with Frankie. Maybe it would all blow over, there were many other days all in the distant memory now but Frankie felt he was unable to shake things off the way he used to. It was like his head had been changed to a different gear and switching it off was more and more difficult. Still for now he would enjoy the lime light and reap the praises of his comrades. Tomorrow would be different. Tomorrow he would be all alone with his own thoughts to contend with. That would be the biggest fight.

8

Liars Bar

Star Wars he answered with a half-cocked smile full of nostalgia and embarrassment. Bradshaw half smiled back as though Frankie had given the perfect answer. Mr. Bradshaw asked about Frankie's life before alcohol as though it was the real mystery. Star Wars was the first thing Frankie remembered capturing his attention and reeling him in to the point of obsession. At primary school he would watch the films over and over on old VHS tapes and practically knew the script. He could whistle along to the classical music creating an atmosphere worthy of the other worlds in a galaxy far far away. It was to be the first thing he collected and craved more and more of. Every spare penny of pocket money or at Christmas and Birthdays he would add to his growing collection of figures and space vehicles. Han Solo, Luke Sky Walker, Boba Fet. Even Princess Lia in her sparkling gold bikini was there. Though this was way before Carrie Fisher chained up in her underwear meant anything other than a toy as his hormones had yet to kick in and start another yearning. Frankie attempted to explain to Bradshaw what this had meant to him as a child and only now as an adult could he see that he struggled to do anything by halves as there were plenty kids of his generation into Star Wars but maybe not quite as whole heartedly as he had been. Next came BMX bikes. Frankie had been given a cheapo silver BMX for Christmas and he had customized it by adding checkered padding and various stickers and accessories and rode it round the street in his little gang as though peacocks showing off their plumage. Frankie went everywhere on his BMX and it brought out a competitive side in all the kids after that Christmas. Who had the most expensive bike? Who could do the best tricks? Who could pull the longest wheelie? Who was the bravest at jumps? Frankie loved the excitement of it all and the bright chrome bikes they rode as though some outlaw motorbike gang they had seen on the telly.

Thinking back, it felt as though one weekend Frankie put down his BMX and somebody handed him a bottle of cider the next and he had again found something else to be obsessed about. He must have been thirteen at the time. The shine left BMX bikes that moment and it seemed like the world glowed in a whole new way. Like Keyser Soze in that movie….childhood was gone.

Now barely teenagers they were playing adult games with the body and minds of children trying to act like big men. The same competition with the BMX's was now who could handle their drink, who could get served at the corner shop, who had tasted what. It was as though some were being fast tracked into dysfunction with the end game being an early grave, prison, unemployment or domestic violence and if you were really lucky you got the full shabang. Others would grow out of drink when the love of a good woman came along. Cider was the gateway but in no time the bar was open and in was vodka, cans, sherry and strawberry wine. Tonic wine always the pinnacle of the teenage drinker and how much they knew the game. Carrying the bottle like a badge of honour the way an oxford graduate would be proud of his degree.

Frankie had always felt that some of his issues had come from poor choices in life and he carried the shame that went with it but under the microscope it became clear that he had no choice. What 13-year-old could stand firm in the face of peer pressure and be the odd one out? Surely, we all wanted to feel part of, and not an outsider? The peer pressure wasn't him having anything pushed on him but he simply wanted to be connected. Not be any different to the friends he went to school with. It seems idealistic as an adult seeing how maybe boxing, football the right girlfriend or some other distraction may have delayed the inevitable for some time but it seemed his path was written in the stars. He knew and had seen little else since he had left the womb but adults drinking and it seemed a goal even to be part of the adult world even although he had witnessed out and out alcoholism first hand. He never thought he would succumb to its grip and always felt he was above it. Was he though?

Frankie even hated the sound of the word alcoholic but knew deep down his Father deserved the label for sure as he drank daily and his behaviour under the influence was off the wall to say the least. He never missed a shift though and their house was clean and tidy with a dinner on the table every night. Surely alcoholics didn't hold down jobs, clean the house and shower every morning. Alcoholics were Jakeys. Wee men in long coats and creased suits, Fag doubts hanging out big beards. Wee men the world didn't give a fuck about. The pest in the local pub who put a damper on the other men's drinking.

Never in a million years did Frankie fall into that category but why then was he sitting here in front of a counsellor trying to find the silver bullet cure for his drinking binges and a racing brain he couldn't control? Maybe he fucked his head up during the rave years all those jacks and jills must have killed off half his brain cells but why then did so many others seem unaffected? Was the piper being paid now for the ecstasy he had felt in the past so many times on the dance floor? He felt singled out and victimised. A pity party for one he couldn't pull himself out of. Poor me another drink.

When Bradshaw approached Frankie's drinking during the sessions it felt raw and his defences were up. He would quickly tell Bradshaw that he was able to stay off the drink for weeks, months even and it didn't bother him. The list rolled off his tongue. I have always worked, I own my own flat, even my pants are Armani! Everybody else is popping pills, taking Charlie and drinking and all I do is drink so fuckin leave me alone! He hated that he could sense Bradshaw's inner smile as he kept a calm exterior calmly nodding encouraging Frankie to go on. Bradshaw said very little and it was as though Frankie was arguing with himself. He could literally feel his argument getting weaker and was almost forced to turn his focus inward and peek under his own mask. Alright he could stay off the drink for long periods but was he ever really free of it even during these periods of abstinence? He always had a great motivator to start a period of sobriety. Fear. The terror he subjected himself to following a night out that had grown into a weekend bender. Coming too in the familiar foetal position dreading even opening his eyes to inspect the devastation he had left around him. The last had him thinking his motor had been stolen from outside the flat then he regained a glimmer of memory that he had driven up the toon to get more drink at some point. He had no recollection of where the motor was when he sobered up and it took him 12 hours to find is safely parked on side street near the cross unscathed. During the search his mind tortured him that he had written it off, knocked a wean over, sold it. He simply didn't know and when he was on it anything was possible. The lost motor incident had him swear off it again and the panic easily kept him sober for the first two weeks. He was really just marking time though until his next drink and the next incident. Sometimes he could drink all night and keep control. The company was good. The vibe just right. He chased the feeling of getting home early morning having satisfied every urge and at times he literally walked into the sunset holding hands with his dream girl, the birds singing in the sky. But these nights were now becoming a distant memory, a thing of the past, it seemed like drink and him were like a weird game of Russian Roulette and every time he was stepping out into the world on a Friday night, he was spinning the barrel of the gun. When he was young the gun rarely had any bullets in it and he usually walked off into the sunset. As drink seemed to consume him sometimes, he would spin that barrel and Bang! He would wake up in a Police cell. All would be well again for a bit and Bang! Another bullet in the gun and he would get bottled in a fight. As he was getting older the gun had more and more bullets and never seemed to click empty. Every drink he was playing with a loaded gun and it was just his luck how big the bang would be. Sometimes if he was lucky it might just be a dose of guilt remorse and shame after a drink. Others it would mean his current relationship was over or he had written a motor off he just couldn't predict or control it. The weird thing is he was well aware of this gamble that went on but somehow it still sucked him into its murky world and a twisted part of him thrived on the adventure of it all.

After the first two weeks off it he would become obsessed with "staying off the drink", make big announcements in work every Monday morning that he was now off it 3 weeks, 4 weeks and so on. His workmates would smile and look at him oddly as he over shared making himself vulnerable to gossip which would fuel his paranoia even further. He would avoid his mates at all cost and barricade himself into the flat watching telly through the night. He made big plans of living a different life, but he knew deep down he was always too nervous to tackle anything. The thought of taking a woman out sober terrified him. He thought about bigger and better jobs but interviews caused him to panic. He felt in a limbo world where he literally couldn't get over himself. He couldn't live with drink or without it. Life without booze seemed boring somehow. Inevitably he would pick up again. Sometimes he could white knuckle it for 8 weeks, 10 weeks. Then the money would build up in the bank the panic would subside and he would bump into an old mate and they would ask if he fancied a quick pint? Sure, what harm could it do? and Bang! The gun would go off again as he would come to days later as his mate went home for dinner safe and sound after 2 pints. He was left scratching his head wondering what happened.

Bradshaw asked him a very simple question. Why do you drink? Or was he making a statement in the face of all the evidence Frankie had given? Frankie attempted to answer anyway. Everybody drinks he stated. I have always drunk. What else is there to do? At least I don't take drugs anymore. Truth, is he felt the shame rising in him as he tried to justify something he struggled to justify even to himself? It's not that he liked drinking as such it was just that he couldn't cope very well when he wasn't drinking. It seemed since the rave days his nerves were shattered all the time and he was quick to anger. During his sober days there was like a build-up of anxiety in him and the only thing that calmed it down was the release that came with the ease and comfort only his old friend alcohol could give. The release seemed almost worth the game of Russian roulette and slight chance that he could still walk off into the sunset with his dream girl. An Angel sent to save Frankie from himself. Somehow remove him from this world he had created and make a man of him. Take him to a place of safety where he could sleep in peace and let go. Just let go of everything. The constant worry. Caring about what they were saying about him. Who was after him? What bad news the postman brought in those envelopes he was afraid to open every morning. Was he going to get sacked from work? When were the Police coming to the door? Feeling hyper sensitive and defensive during even the most mundane conversations in work and feeling everyone was talking down to him and he had to defend his position constantly. It just went on and on and the only rest bite he ever got was when he was drunk.

It was like letting the air out of a tight balloon on a Friday and he could finally relax. Two or three drinks in he began to feel normal and by the fourth he just didn't give a fuck about anything. He finally became at peace with the world and nothing scared or intimidated him any longer. Hardest thing was most people couldn't see through him and they thought he was naturally like this and he had the added pressure of keeping up the façade when he was sober but he would lose face and shite it to ask a girl out sober and it was like he could no longer stick up for himself properly without sweating and stuttering. It was like drink had given him the wings to fly but then taken away the sky.

As the session was nearing the end Bradshaw handed Frankie a leaflet and asked him to look at it for next week and do his best to answer honestly. Frankie agreed and took the leaflet and put it in the inside pocket of his jacket telling Bradshaw he would do his homework like a good little boy or at least that was how it felt.

Here are 20 Questions designed to help you determine how alcohol has affected your life.

1. Do you lose time from work due to drinking?
2. Is drinking making your home life unhappy?
3. Do you drink because you are shy with other people?
4. Is drinking affecting your reputation?
5. Have you ever felt remorse after drinking?
6. Have you got into financial difficulties as a result of drinking?
7. Do you turn to lower companions and an inferior environment when drinking?
8. Does your drinking make you careless of your family's welfare?
9. Has your ambition decreased since drinking?
10. Do you crave a drink at a definite time daily?
11. Do you want a drink the next morning?
12. Does drinking cause you to have difficulty sleeping?
13. Has your efficiency decreased since drinking?
14. Is drinking jeopardizing your job or business?
15. Do you drink to escape from worries or trouble?
16. Do you drink alone?
17. Have you ever had a complete loss of memory as a result of drinking?

18. Has your physician ever treated you for drinking?

19. Do you drink to build up your self-confidence?

20. Have you ever been to a hospital or institution on account of drinking?

If you have answered YES to any of the questions, there is a definite warning that you may be alcoholic. If you have answered YES to any 2, the chances are that you are an alcoholic. If you have answered YES to 3 or more, you are definitely an alcoholic.

How many questions did YOU answer YES to?

Frankie felt both ashamed and relieved as he read through the questions back at the flat nodding in agreeance to 18 out of 20. Best test score he had had in years he thought. But was drink his problem or was it his solution? He had always thought that he had some undiagnosed mental health condition, an oversight on the part of the NHS and one day a new doctor would recognise that he had ADHD all his life or some other disorder and hand him the prescription containing the one a day tablet that would make it all better. The mythical silver bullet no less. One tablet that would make it all better. He would get the label he was looking for, all would be well and he might even get a bit of sympathy at how difficult life had been on him. But Alcoholic that was the last label anybody wanted. What was an alcoholic anyway? Did Alkeys no need to drink 24/7 or they took fits or some weird seizure? Did they no drink Tenants Super and turps? He was never like that and he was always immaculately dressed so he couldn't be an alcoholic. Could he? He felt sure that his relationship with drink was not like everybody else's and he was always greedy with drink even when he was a boy but alcoholic seemed a bit extreme and the title seemed even more embarrassing than being a pisshead, steamer, booze bag and all the other colourful names he had heard him being referred to with at least some fondness the way a king may laugh at a court jester. Maybe Frankie was getting sick of being looked at as a joke and his reputation slowly crumbling around him with his self-respect. He yearned for a life of calm and respectability but could never seem to get off the starting blocks. Christ did he even know where the starting blocks were?

He had peeked into the world of respectability on several occasions when he had made half arsed attempts at settling down when he had met the right girl. Frankie would run towards love like a wean who had lost his mother in a supermarket and finding her made him feel safe for a while at least. The pattern was always much the same. Frankie would meet a girl who was good looking, this mattered a lot to him not just to appeal to his sexual urges but he was always concerned about others opinion and if he could be slagged if his latest conquest was too fat or not up to his high standards. He would reel her in by showing her his sensitive side and he had the ability to talk about any subject all night long and the initial euphoria of the love vibe seemed to give him some kind of contentment he rarely felt. The relationship was always intense to the point of obsession and he would spend every night with his latest victim during the initial period and his drinking would be firmly on the back burner. Every now and then he would have a mad night with his mates but completely tone it down when he was with the current soulmate. He would tell them stuff like I am going down to Tommy's to watch the football on Saturday and make it all sound so normal and civilised and he would be at Tommy's alright but no football was on and the mob in the living room was like a minibus heading to community service had emptied Haddow's and set up camp. All would be well with the lads and Frankie would make some effort to get home on the Sunday at least. Through his fear and paranoia, he would tell the lucky lady that they had a six pack and some pizza the night before as though he was living in an episode of Happy Days in North Lanarkshire making it all seem so normal where underneath the whole façade he struggled with guilt and anxiety.

Now and then on nights on the town with girls he would get drunker than he planned and they would put it down to a one-off mad night. Frankie knew though that his mask was slipping and he was beginning to show his true colours. Nights in at the weekend were becoming boring. Somehow just not really in his nature somehow. At times he would get itchy feet and he felt the call of the wild. A longing to chase some kind of excitement. The initial euphoria of love would lessen and his dream girl would fall off the pedestal he had put her on and suddenly appear human. He would see her then with all her faults and imperfections and somehow the shine would dull and he would stop caring half as much. Then he would feel smothered or just lacked enthusiasm. He would play with the idea of ending it for a bit in his head and when he built up enough courage, he would finish it without and real explanation. How could he have been so in love and so keen but then suddenly walk away leaving so many questions unanswered for them? It seemed he had gone all in within weeks to game over overnight, sometimes it took months others a couple of years but the result was always the same. He would just change his mind overnight. The truth is he didn't like hurting other people and he assumed they were all as sensitive as he was. He just couldn't do it, no matter how hard he tried or how badly they had treated him.

It's not like he had a type but he could see there were usually a pattern he followed in his relationships mainly he would meet some girl who was high on the looks department but would have red flags all over her which Frankie would totally ignore. He would be besotted by this princess and adore her despite her obvious red flags such as her single parent status, various financial issues, crazy ex-boyfriend, addictions etc etc. He would feel like he could easily fix all these issues by throwing money at them or setting about the ex. However, by the time his rose-tinted specs had fallen off he would see the princess as just another single parent living in the high flats struggling to get by with her big bag of issues and he would suddenly feel sick at his naivety and her humanity not meeting up to his unachievable standards. This realisation would be his queue to bail. As usual with no real explanation.

Then he would be rescued by some Angel who would shower him with love and there would be some role reversal would take place. Again, he would show his best side but he wouldn't be reeling them in they would be making all the moves and he would be led into their safe world they would present to him and he would feel loved and secure. As time went on though some of the old feelings would come back, feeling smothered, under pressure all the time being nagged constantly about trivial things like his smoking! Here he was living his healthiest life, cutting down the drink never in any trouble and would get constant grief about his ten a day Benson habit. They had maybe seen some good in him and would try and mould him into something they envisioned as their perfect partner as though he wasn't good enough in the here and now but a future version of him who didn't smoke, earned more money, had nicer friends, wore different clothes. Again, the constant pressure got to him and he would walk without very little explanation. With no real idea of the devastation, he was leaving behind him. He felt free of the pressure while she was left heart broken. His inability to communicate hurt her more than the truth.

Once he thought he had found the one and as was the norm it was fireworks from the word go and he seen her as some kind of Angel. Her position of superiority in the relationship was quickly established as she would continually remind him of her looks, popularity, being part of the in crowd etc etc. Her main topic of conversation would be herself or her long list of ex's making Frankie increasingly insecure and having to work harder and harder to keep her happy and feed her narcissistic needs. At the time he was totally unaware of any of this however and only realised with the gift on hind sight that every bit of constant reinforcement of her superiority had come from her lips and he had fell for it hook line and sinker. The relationship felt like he was there to serve her and ensure her happiness all at the expense of any happiness he once possessed. He had been conned into feeling her every infidelity and selfish behaviour was solely his responsibility and he just couldn't cut the mustard. Until they finished and he began to receive the tearful phone calls from her and suddenly she not only appeared human to him but someone far more fragile than he ever was and he felt a fool for never having seen it. It was back to the booze and dreaming of his perfect lover who would make it all alright. He would be back living in his murky world dreaming of the day when love would find a way. Like in the songs he had listened too since those first 7-inch singles he played on loop just as girls started to catch his young eye.

Frankie was already dreading next week's session with Bradshaw and thought he might lie about the homework. Maybe he would tell him he had just forgot it or answered No to every question but one thing was for sure no way was he giving him the satisfaction of calling Frankie an Alcoholic. Specky cunt.

9

I don't like Mondays

His eyes scanned across the packed wardrobe as he slid the door fully open to reveal shirts of every colour, material and check. Normally Frankie could pick clothes almost instinctively but today was different. Today he would face a panel of jobs worth cunts who would be judging him from their ivory towers. He had to give the right impression. The impression that he was taking this back to work interview seriously but he didn't want to look too sharp as though he had his shit together, he was off long-term sick with stress. A position so familiar with half the employees of North Lanarkshire Council that it didn't worry Frankie too much but his hand had to be played just right to gain the sympathy of the panel while he hid behind the employment law which protected the chancers who fitted in so well with the council. He knew they had to jump through hoops to show they had been fair with him these days as he had pulled the classic move to declaring he was suffering from anxiety and depression all confirmed by a pink sick note handed in every four weeks. Truth, is he had taken off so many Mondays on the sick and ran out of excuses for his constant lateness that he was fearing the worst for his job. True his nerves were shattered half the time but work was becoming something that he found harder and harder to muster up any motivation for so he hit the pause button and went off sick to allow him to sort things out. He thought he would treat the period off work as a period of recuperation, where he could make the changes and get himself back on track. Turns out he had spent most of it in the boozer or lying in his bed. He opted for a button-down shirt and cords, keeping it casual but smart. He got dressed in no time and headed into the civic where he was to meet some head of HR he had rarely seen before even although he had worked there for nearly ten years. There was a mutual understanding during the interview that both he and the arsehole from HR were going through the motions and Frankie knew the script too well to say anything incriminating. He told the guy that he may benefit from the counselling they offered and would consider a phased return when he felt well enough. Frankie almost clicked his heals as he left the building knowing all was well with his job and he was on safe ground. The anxiety he felt before going in vanished and he now considered taking the full six months off full pay before he went back. He knew he was good at his job when he went in and was on form but he just couldn't find any enthusiasm for it these days. Office work appealed to him leaving school in the late 80s as he liked the idea of going to work in a suit and tie and maybe driving a flash car to the office besides that he hated getting his hands dirty. Like a Scottish version of Wall Street minus the braces. Reality kicked in pretty quick when he entered the government Youth Training Scheme as an office clerk earning £29.50 a week. He struggled to get through the week never mind get the Armani Suit and brief case. He drifted from department to department the wages increasing only slightly and found himself in Welfare Rights. An honourable occupation, man of the people. Held high in some circles as though he was fighting the good fight for the common man. Truth is though Frankie didn't share these values and it grated on him at times how he had worked all his life while filling form after form for the work shy and the lazy who seemed to be in the pub most days. He saw no honour in it and felt used by them. Used to dodge through the system unscathed as the genuine cases seemed in the minority. He would listen to bar room philosophers waxing lyrical about communism and equality for all but Frankie couldn't understand how anybody was cool with freeloading. It was a job to him and a job only. A means to an end. Beer money at the end of the week and that was it. There was a sadness about this as he was approaching thirty and still hadn't quite found his niche in life. Sure, he had always been into music but he was tone deaf and couldn't play a note. He wondered if he would ever find his calling that would one day make him flourish and the world would recognise his uniqueness or would he trudge to the grave in a mundane 9-5. Only time would tell.

Stick in at school was the mantra he heard over and over from his parents and grandparents as though "sticking in" was the golden ticket out the scheme. He was never quite sure what "stickin in" meant and anyhow he had to navigate four or five years through territorial gang wars, bouts of acne, teenage drinking, as well as keeping up the pretence that you knew everything about sex while absolutely shitting yourself to go near any females. He remembers being approached by a lassie in his class and asking him if he would go out with her pal? He instantly refused claiming she was ugly.

But he was scared, scared she would see behind his mask, scared of showing his inexperience to the world, scared of what everyone would say. Was she good looking enough to avoid any slagging's? Looking back the girl in question was lovely in every way it was he who felt inadequate and simply cared too much about what others thought of him. Another missed opportunity down to him caring too much about them.

Frankie resented the world at times, felt like he had lived with one hand tied behind his back. He looked at guys he had grown up with and how they had turned out. They made life look so easy. Got trades, qualifications, wife, weans, big houses, nice motors, holidays in the sun. Financial planning and pensions while Frankie lived wage to wage aimlessly. He knew he wasn't stupid and liked who he was in many ways, but the constant mayhem growing up and the mantra repeated to him over and over by his father that he was a useless cunt had subliminally sunk into him. Anytime he felt like striving for something more he always had a devil on his shoulder telling him that he would never be able to do it. If there was a female he liked and there was a good vibe between them, green lights flashing. He still had a voice saying "She will never go out with you". It was like a glass ceiling he just couldn't smash through unless he was mad with it and the voice stopped.

He only ever started drinking because everybody else was doing it and he didn't want to look like a shitebag. He had seen the states his Father got into most nights and it held little appeal and as for the taste of those Super Lagers. Arghh! Totally disgusting. Cheap cider seemed the thirteen-year-olds starter pack into the adult world of drink and debauchery. In true Frankie fashion from feeling pushed into trying drink and too scared to say no, it no time at all he was the moderator of the weekend mayhem and planned with precision ways and means of getting drink and evading capture by his parents. Before he had even left school, his parents had found him drinking many times and he always felt confused at the hypocrisy of his Father being a daily drinker but would react as though his weekend tipples were an act of treason. He would shout and scream so much he would often wait in the factories across from his house until the early hours until he crept into the house unnoticed avoiding another episode of his father's madness. He even got in the habit of pushing his bed against his room door barricading himself in until the next day when his Father would be sober again and oblivious to his lunacy the previous evening and it would be safe to come out again. His Mother not being the most outgoing character at the best of times would become even more distant as Frankie hit his teenage years and rebelled against the world. The relationship he had with his Parents deteriorated daily as his father drank more and attacked him daily with the conversation narrowed down to one-word answers. "Where are you gaun?" Oot. "Who with?" Nobody. "When you coming back?" Efter "Whits that?" Nothing. This was the extent of the growls between them. Frankie himself started to emulate his mother and began to clam up inside, he was always such an outgoing boy but now fear of judgement and criticism made him pull the shutters down. The communication in the house was child like and the conversation never developed beyond this as the years progressed. It kept his growth at the same level as his parents until he moved out. The constant attack in the house from his father turned him sensitive and he would feel a gentle burn at school if a teacher talked down to him or worse still, he was on the receiving end of a slagging. There were various subject matters you could get slagged for dependant on your appearance e.g. Fat, thin, spotty, red hair, specks etc. But you could also be slagged for something you had done in the past e.g. shat yourself at Primary, kissed a fat lassie, been caught wanking etc. This were standard slagging material but there were also more cruel labels stuck on those with severe afflictions that crossed the line into bullying, generally reserved for the poor or the damaged. It seemed to him that the whole day at school would be spent slagging each other and your ability to give or take a slagging would add to where you were in the pecking order. Frankie had to learn quickly. He soon developed a sharp wit and sharper tongue to avoid the burn of getting a slagging and it worked well making him again appear like jack the lad when inside he was trying hard to suss life out. It was during his teenage years that he began playing different roles. One for in the house – Angelic. One for School – Class Clown. One for football – Hardman. One for the girls – Romantic dreamer. And it caused him mass anxiety if his various worlds were to meet and he would not know who to be that day. All the while appearing to the world that he was full of himself.

Maybe the solution to his teenage confusion was found in the bottle as he soon found his feet in the drinking world and graduated from cheap cider to fortified wines and sherry in no time. The 15% proof providing him with the perfect release from his inhibitions and fears. Allowing him to let go and feel at ease with the world. His problem even back then though was that that he thought that more drink would increase his euphoria but the more he drank the less euphoric he became and he only found oblivion way before he ever sought it. A greedy drinker from day one but there were times when he would wake up soaked by the rain and dirt head to toe in the middle of a graveyard or golf course with no memory of how he got there. All part of the drinking game he thought. This all took place all before he was even legally aged to drink.

Although these episodes lacked enjoyment for Frankie, he quickly shrugged them off and never questioned it much. Maybe the ease and comfort he got from the drink was worth the price though these episodes were few and far between at that age. He mostly enjoyed drink, especially at football where the buzz of the day mixed with the alcohol seemed a match made in heaven. Football violence during this era was a weekly occurrence and he never missed a game home and away. Always hungry for the next experience or tale to tell. He loved the buzz of a Saturday mobbed up in best clobber taking on the world. The feeling was unbeatable and he loved the notoriety of being a Casual. Every Saturday an adventure and a culture which filled his every waking thought. The drinking seemed to add to the notoriety and letting the world know he didn't give a fuck while inside he was tortured by his own mind. His inner world and the life he lived were two different realities.

He wondered if he would be living this life, off sick from a shite job with the council, seeing therapists, nightmares, constant anxiety if he had loving parents like his friends growing up. Parents who made him feel safe, made him feel like he belonged in this world. Somebody to guide him through and give him that feeling that everything was going to be alright that he longed for. Parents like Tommy's Mum and Dad who loved Tommy without condition. Frankie could almost feel the love when he was in their house when they were boys. The air seemed lighter somehow. They laughed together, cared for ach other and looked out for each other while Frankie felt like he lived in the lion's den when he was home. With parents like Tommy's, he could have been somebody. Maybe he still could.

10

Last Orders

Frankie lay deadly silent and still, it was almost like he was playing dead. The familiar Sunday morning fetal position he had lay in so many times before. He could see the sunlight pierce through his eyelids but he refused to open them. He wanted to hold onto the comfort of his bed as long as he could. He just couldn't face the world right now. He knew the world held the all too familiar feeling of guilt and terror and he would need to wade through the next few days before he could almost live with himself again. It was a pattern he had repeated over and over again for years now. He once loved the euphoric feeling he got on a Friday after work and the endless possibilities of fun as the weekend approached and he could forget any responsibility and well and truly let his hair down. Nights out chasing women, singing songs and feeling alive. The process was repeated every Friday and Saturday as standard and memories were created, friendships were formed and hearts were broken. A time for being young and carefree. Sure, sometimes he crossed the line and woke up with more than a hangover to contend with but he had the arrogance of youth on his side and could easily shake it off with a general feeling that "Boys will be Boys". Excess was celebrated and bad behavior rewarded with a further boost to his reputation that he didn't give a fuck and cared for no man.

The arrogance of youth had left him sometime in his mid-twenties, times had changed and so had he. Self-doubt and fear had gotten the better of him somewhere along the line and he had succumbed to its power. The Friday night out he once loved had became the starting blocks for days of oblivion which he would remember little of on the Monday leaving him racked with remorse until he plodded through the week where he would repeat the whole process again praying the destruction would be manageable when it was all over. Enjoyment from booze was now a thing of the past. The drink had become a potion he consumed to stop his mind haunting him and try to fill the whole inside him he could never fill.

He finally opened his eyes stretched his arms, rubbing his face which was rough with a three-day stubble. His mouth was like sandpaper and he had a taste in his mouth that only three days of smoking and drinking could produce. A taste unknown to those outside the life he lived. He looked at the back of his hands and was glad there was no visible sign of cuts or grazes. He sat up in bed and his mind spun in an attempt to figure out what he needed right now. A mind so familiar with want. He walked to the bathroom and pissed like the proverbial race horse. His piss was like Lucozade.

He washed his hands under the freezing cold tap and threw some water over his face in an attempt to get some life in him. He stood in front of the bathroom mirror as he patted his face with the towel. He was directly in front of the mirror as he lowered the towel below his eyes still drying his chin. He froze suddenly as he looked into his own eyes, he seen his Father staring straight back at him. It rattled him. He hated no one like he hated his own Father but he couldn't deny the resemblance. It literally stared him straight in the face. Was he like his father in more ways than just his looks he though? No, he though, was he? His Father was an alcoholic and a bully. Frankie was no bully but was his drinking so different now he had grown up a wee bit? The though shook him to the core, it was like a peek into the truth. The lies he had been telling himself were dissolving and he was having a moment of clarity he did not want. He felt sick as the feeling shook his guts.

In an attempt to break his thoughts, he walked to the kitchen feeling the cold floor tiles under his bare feet he opened the fridge looking for something wet to drink. There was little more than a light in his fridge so it would have to be good old tap water. He let the tap run for a minute and filled his mug over and over as he poured water into his system like a man lost in the desert. He took the last cigarette from his packet and lit up feeling the nicotine rush through his veins he began the tribunal of piecing together the previous few days.

He remembered leaving the flat on Friday arranging to meet Tommy in The Tavern around dinner time. All was well and they drank pints steady as the pub filled up with those on their weekly night out. He remembered the point where he was glowing with the booze and had that happy couldn't care less glow he craved. He mingled in the pub with folk from school and they left there a few hours later but there didn't seem to be much to be concerned about. Tick…all well in The Tavern.

He then remembers going to Haddow's and stocking up on drink and jumping in a taxi which took them to a mate of Tommy's in the towers. Frankie had a good drink in him when they arrived in the flat but again, he didn't seem to remember anything to be concerned about, he knew most in the flat and oblivion was the norm there. Tick…no concerns in the towers.

He walked back to his bedroom to lie back in bed and trawl for more stuff to be paranoid about. His clothes were on the bedroom floor in a bundle on top of his trainers which were covered in mud. He lifted his cords and looked through the pockets. Wallet still there with a big bundle of change in the right pocket and the left pocket had a twenty pack of cigarettes with one in it plus a clipper lighter. His cords looked in one piece. He then lifted the Paul and Shark polo and tutted to himself as he noticed it was ripped near the buttons. He was initially gutted at the loss of the polo shirt then he worried at how the damaged happened as he had zero recollection.

He remembers daylight Saturday morning heading back over to the shop for more cans laughing and joking with the lads but there after he remembered nothing until about 12 hours after that when he was back in the boozer later on Saturday night and it was dark outside. His next memory is coming into the flat and sitting alone listening to music and drinking a bottle of Newcastle and had no idea where he got it from as he hated the stuff.

He felt that limbo land feeling he had where he felt tears would almost well up inside him but they never came, he wished there was a shell he could crawl inside to hide away from the world he feared so much when he was in this condition. He hoped the dull ache in his stomach would ween soon. It would normally go the next day but there were times it clung to him for days reminding him of the fool he had been the previous bender. He had heard many times from ex-girlfriends or his mother that he was such a lovely guy when sober but drink changed him beyond recognition. He had always brushed it off feeling nagged or that they were manipulating him to change somehow. The truth was sinking in through his pores now and he was struggling to believe his own lies anymore.

Where had he been and who with? Frankie was a social guy particularly when he was drunk but he had a strange habit of going off on his own and looking for excitement elsewhere if he wasn't finding it in the place his friends were. It had gotten worse since he had been single again as if he was always hunting for that Angel again who would save him from himself and make him feel a little more complete and bring him back in line

Should he go out and face the music, see if he would get a reaction from anyone or they could fill him in on what had happened or just brave it out in the flat until he got his wits about him again? He stared blankly at the ceiling and released all the air from his lungs and turned on his side again. Just lying there waiting for it to come tumbling down on top of him.

Frankie shook off the dull feeling a little and hit the shower. The steaming hot water started to cleanse him on the outside at least. He got himself dressed and went round the flat emptying ashtrays, binning anything that was lying around the flat in an attempt to restore some order in his life. He looked at the Paul & Shark polo and decided it was beyond repair and he stuffed it in the plastic bag he was using to clean up. He exhaled at the loss of the Polo, it wasn't so much the money and although it had cost him a few quid but more the fact he had fucked up something he cared about again through drink. Yet another fuck up he thought to himself.

He was down to the last cigarette he found in his pocket and decided to brave the walk to the shop to get more as there was no way he was getting through the day without any. He might check the cashline too and assess the financial damage of the last few days. He hoped he would avoid anyone he had met over the weekend with the usual "you were in some state last night" banter as though he was unaware of the nick he was in as much as they were unaware of the impact it had on him. Some still believed the lie he was immune to life and that he was handling this.

In the shop he got the usual twenty Benson and some orange Lucozade. He would phone a takeaway later if hunger came upon him but right now his guts were filled with guilt. Waiting in line in the shop he looked at the drink packed shelves next to him filled with every kind of booze known to man. There were times before he would mentally pick stuff for his next session. I would start with that sherry, then get a few becks, maybe some of that brandy there etc etc. Truth is though he was becoming scared to drink he just couldn't predict his behavior and was remembering less and less and any ability he once had to handle it was dwindling. It was like an old lover he kept seeking comfort in but broke his heart every time but he couldn't find the strength to stay away from her.

He walked from the shop slowly stopping every few steps to swig some Lucozade letting the gas tingle his throat and give him some kind of taste in his mouth. He lit a cigarette and walked on feeling slightly more human now. He felt his phone vibrate in his pocket and pulled it out looking at the name on the tiny Nokia screen. Tommy. His partner in crime since they were boys but right now, he couldn't face talking to him and put the phone back in his pocket letting the vibrations end. Frankie walked another ten minutes and was nearing the flat again when he felt the vibrate once more. Tommy again. He instantly wanted to switch the phone off but the paranoia at what Tommy wanted so urgently got the better of him and he decided to front it and answer. Alright mate? Tommy sighed on the other end of the phone. Alright? What the fuck was that all about last night? You aff yer heed. What? Frankie replied with no idea of what Tommy meant. Can you not remember Tommy asked in disbelief?

Tommy went onto relay the story of the previous evening when the two were well in party mode and all was well until Frankie messed it up. It seems they were walking past The Miners Club in good spirits laughing and joking as per usual when Frankie like a dog out of trap two sprinted towards an old guy leaving the Miners and started windmilling punches at him. The old guy cowering and shouting Sorry over and over as Tommy pulled Frankie back the old guy took his hands down from his Face. He knew him. It was Frankie's old man. Tommy got Frankie out of the way quickly and told him that Frankie was in tears with rage and ran off down the street and that was the last Tommy had seen him. Frankie knew nothing of this but it explained the ripped polo shirt and the guilt hanging over him.

Frankie's old man was sixty now and the drink had taken its toll on him. He had rarely seen him in the last few years since his mother had passed away. The months following the funeral he would pop in some days after work out of some sense of weird duty even although he hated the man. He felt he should for some reason. Eventually he just couldn't face it. He would dread going into see him and it would waste his whole day with the prospect of the visit ahead. When he left him, he felt like there was a dark cloud hanging over him. The visits became fortnightly, then monthly, then …he just stopped going.

What had he done? Had he kicked fuck out of him? His own Father. Had anyone else seen him? Throwing punches at an old guy. Although his old man was only sixty his years of drink had made him look older. Had Frankie let his anger get the better of him and taken a liberty? Just like his father had with him so many times when he was a defenseless wee boy? What would his mother think of him if she was still alive? What would everyone say about him? Under the influence of the drink none of these worries would have concerned Frankie and he would have felt just in his actions towards his old man. He had fantasized so many times of giving his old man what he deserved. Giving the wee boy inside Frankie his shot of the title and seeing if his old man had what it took against a man not a wee boy. He suspected his old man was the type who was spoken down to in work or in the boozer as few had time for him. He was the type of coward who would come home and even up the score a wee bit by taking it out on the wife or battering the weans. Frankie felt more than hate towards his father, it was disgust. Disgust at the type of human he was and shame that he was connected to him. Now he was becoming him. Frankie shuddered at the thought.

Tommy kept talking on the other end of the phone but Frankie's head was still milling over what Tommy had told him. He told Tommy he would phone him back later and headed to the flat to hide until he could process this a wee bit. He pushed his feelings aside an told himself "Fuck him, he got what he deserved the old bastard". It just wasn't washing with him though. He felt remorse and couldn't deny it. His old man did deserve it and much more if the truth be told. Not like this though this was far from Karma or any type of justice. This was merely Frankie repeating the same behavior his old man had displayed so many times before. Frankie realized that maybe he wasn't like his old man as his old man seemed to be devoid of guilt or any kind of conscience. If Frankie didn't change his ways, he would just be repeating the same cycle over and over again right through the generations. It got him thinking about how his old man was treated when he was a boy as he never knew anything about his fathers upbringing. Maybe his old man had been a victim of life once.

Right now, his head was working overtime on him and he got back to the safety of the flat. He locked the door and removed the key as usual and dipped the blinds. He would need to hibernate for a bit to sort his head out and let the disturbance in his mind calm a wee bit before he tackled this. He was in no fit state to face the world. He switched off the Nokia. If the Police came to the door, he would blank it. The next day or two would be spent in isolation, the prospect of which terrified him but it was a lot better than facing the realities of the world outside.

11

My name is

Frankie peered around the smoke-filled room from under the skip of his baseball cap trying his best to remain under the radar. Head bowed scarf pulled up over his chin. At twenty-nine he seemed to be one of the youngest in the dingy old church hall where the group almost cuddled into the polystyrene cups of tea and coffee they held as they sucked hard on roll ups and king size cigarettes. The group faced towards the table at the front which housed two speakers as though some kind of religious ceremony was about to take place. The hall felt totally alien to him but strangely he felt at home here.

It had been nearly a week since Frankie had come off the most recent bender and the incident with his father haunted him on top of the oh so familiar fragile nerves. He still hadn't managed to shake off that feeling of impending doom hanging over him as though the bad news was in the post and his world would soon feel the devastation. The not knowing and waiting sometimes worse than anything that would come his way. He was nowhere near ready to approach his old man and try to sort this mess out or if he ever would be. Right now, he felt he would avoid him for life but just hoped he didn't make things worse on his next session.

This pivotal moment in Frankie's young life seemed like the ultimate paradox. Here he was at rock bottom suffering the shame of walking through the doors of Alcoholics Anonymous not knowing that having the courage to put one foot in front of the other into this dingy little room would be the best move he would ever make though right now he felt lower than a snake's belly button. He knew he was at a crossroads in his life and if nothing changed, he knew the writing was on the wall. He scanned the room for the alcoholics. The middle-aged woman who had served him the tea seemed clean, tidy and cheery and he though she must be a volunteer from the church. There were two other guys at the front in suits who were deep in conversation and Frankie thought they may be Social Workers or some kind of therapist. There was a guy about forty next to Frankie in jeans and a denim jacket with long hair and a beard and Frankie thought he was a shoe in to be an Alky. He could imagine him holding court in any pub in Scotland quite comfortable in the roll of bar room philosopher. He seemed a man with a story to tell. However, Frankie felt the others mainly just normal looking folk of various shapes and sizes. A bell was rung from the table as though last orders were about to be shouted and the room went deathly silent as though the audience well-schooled in the process. The guy on the left at the table began by saying, "Good evening, everyone my name is Gordon and I am an alcoholic." Frankie smiled inside as though he had been transported to the set of some Hollywood movie as he had heard this being said in films but he wasn't sure if it happened in real life. The next half hour or so passed quickly as the two guys spoke about what life was like when they were drinkers and the carnage the booze had caused in their lives but

Frankie didn't really take much in. His head was all over the place and he couldn't hold a thought for more than a minute and he sat there daydreaming and scanning his anxious brain for stuff he should be worrying about. It was his default setting.

The feeling of paranoia and shame he was carrying was no stranger to him. He had felt it many times before. Times where he had made a monumental fuck up while mad with it and carried the shame of the incident until he could live with himself again. This was different though. Although he had consumed his body weight in booze many times before and had lived with his own guilt, attacking his own Father had been a new low. He was quite simply sick of feeling sick and could no longer trust himself when drunk never mind anybody else. Waking up consumed by fear having bounced off his hallway walls as he dragged himself to bed after two days on it. He just couldn't do it anymore. The months leading up to this night had seen him promise himself time and time again that he was going to get his act together and get off the booze. Maybe hit the gym. Buy some nice clothes. Balance the scales in favour of positivity and make him feel a little better about himself like he done so many times before. He once went 13 weeks without a drop passing his lips and the monk like existence had its benefits. He always had money in his pocket, a full fridge and he could look himself in the eye when he was shaving in the mirror. Lately though he lacked something. He lacked the motivation to make the changes and the drink kept pulling him back in. Every other Monday morning he would make plans to get off it next weekend but sometimes before Thursday was out he would be back on it and the drink was beginning to call the shots. Maybe the incident with his old man had forced him into taking the action he so needed.

Here he was at a meeting of Alcoholics Anonymous before he was even thirty. Hardly something he had on his bucket list. Though strangely under the cloak and dagger of it all, driving 15 miles away from home to avoid detection, hat and scarf on in a poor disguise, it felt somehow the right thing to do. As Frankie had approached his late twenties the fun of drinking had somehow faded. It was like a thorn in his side now. Something in his life that was well and truly holding him back. Without the booze he could make steady progress at times. He was disciplined even. He had trained and kept fit most of his life but his weekend benders would fuck all that up. He never struggled to get to the gym or get out and run like so many complained about the lack of motivation. He was the opposite he needed to train. He suffered mild guilt if he didn't, but with booze in the mix it was one step forward two steps back and he was always playing catch up with his recent progress taking a hit. His work life was the same he could go in feeling confident and do the work with his eyes closed and he felt confident with the punters but spending half his week pished had taken its toll on him and he was phoning in sick more and more often or running in late in the morning making up excuse after excuse. The need to lie to the work was adding to his anxiety and the para feeling he had when he was there. It was like he was always waiting on that tap on the shoulder to tell him the boss wanted to see him now. The tap never came but the feeling never left him. He was drinking every penny and he hated the beans on toast mentality he had to adopt until next pay day or tap money from any acquaintance in the boozer to keep him in beer. He was just fuckin sick of the whole rigmarole of the world of drink.

When the two guys at the table finished speaking the meeting stopped for more tea and coffee and the room was again ablaze with cigarette smoke. The atmosphere was warm and friendly and Frankie felt safe in here, though his unfamiliarity must have shown as he was approached by an old guy with white hair who asked him if it was his first meeting? Frankie nodded in agreement but for a man who could normally talk for Scotland it seemed like he had lost his tongue. The old guy sat in the orange plastic chair next to him and began reassuring Frankie he was in the right place and gave him some friendly advice though very little stuck to Frankie as his thoughts still raced but he was glad that he had at least managed to utter a few words to someone else in the room. The old guy gave Frankie a handful of leaflets and wee cards with bits of advice when committing to sobriety and Frankie stuffed them in his pocket agreeing that he would come back to another meeting soon and he meant it but the old guy was keen to meet the next night but Frankie told him there was no need as he only ever drank at weekends and the old guy just smiled and they shook hands agreeing to meet the following Friday at yet another church hall.

The others in the room then went onto speak individually for a few minutes each and Frankie was blown away when each and every one of them introduced themselves as "an alcoholic". His previous assessment that the clean, tidy and confident in the room were all in the care field was totally wrong and it seemed the whole room was full of recovering alcoholics some with years and years off the drink. This intrigued Frankie and he felt more and more that maybe his place was among these people. Even at the end when they stood up and said a short prayer before leaving it still didn't put him off though he would usually run a mile at the mention of the word God never mind pray.

This place could be just what he was looking for but Alcoholic? Surely, he wasn't an Alcoholic.

The next few days Frankie's head buzzed with it all and the feeling of guilt and shame was dimmed a bit by the excitement of this place he had found that might contain the answers he was always looking for. Like the missing piece of the jigsaw. He found it hard in work not to spill the beans and tell everyone where he had been and where he was going again that Friday. It was a bit like his teenage years when he found ecstasy and would be in work acting straight and normal when he would be part of this underground world at the weekends. Had he found a new underground world that would lead to happier times? He hoped so and his gut told him he was on the right path though he worried about how he would be seen by everyone going to these weird meetings and saying he was an Alcoholic. Fuck them he thought he was doing this. It felt right.

He felt a little more comfortable on the Friday night as

he walked into the church hall. He was welcomed with open arms. As he took his place in the queue for the tea and coffee the old guy with the white hair approached him again with a smile from ear to ear. Glad you could make it son! He said and shook his hand with a vice like grip. The two then stood at the edge of the room and the old guy asked him how he was? Frankie felt a million times better than he had the previous week and was starting to get his wits about him a wee bit. He told the old guy that he was sick of the booze and over the last couple of years he had tried time and time again to pack it in himself but he just kept going back on it without any real reason. He told the old guy about the counselling which helped but couldn't stop him from drinking. Frankie told the old guy that he got a good vibe from the meetings but he didn't think he was an alcoholic. The old guy smiled. You don't need to be to be here, you only need an honest desire to stop drinking. This made Frankie feel a bit better and the two sat together and again listened to the speakers at the table at the front of the room.

Frankie felt a little more of what was said was sinking in and when he left that night, he thought about the explanation the guy speaking had given in relation to alcoholism. He told the room that some people had a different reaction to alcohol to others and some when they put alcohol into their system, they set up a craving. A craving for alcohol which could not be quenched. Quite simply he said, "One drink was too many and a million was not enough." This made total sense to Frankie as each and every time he tried to control his drink he simply couldn't. He has tried cutting out cheap wine, not drinking spirits, going down the pub with limited money, going down the pub at 10pm, drinking in quieter pubs, drinking in different company. The result was always the same though as soon as he got the taste for it he was on a mission for oblivion. There were many times where he had important stuff in his life that had mattered too him and he would go for a quick pint and the job interview the next day or whatever he had planned was a no go as he would still be on the booze. Time and time again he had promised girlfriends he would meet them and he would promise himself he would have just a few pints and again he would disappear as soon as he started drinking and let them down. Sometimes he would be missing for days. It didn't seem to matter how important the event or the person, drink won every time as soon as the first one passed his lips.

This philosophy of not lifting the first drink sat well with him. It meant the mind games and constantly trying to control consumption was over. If he didn't touch one, he didn't set up this craving. He felt relieved that he had finally learnt this but stupid at the same time as it had taken this long as he had always seemed to drink this way from the word go. He had tried everything to control his drinking except actually not drinking! It maddened him at times when he watched guys, he grew up with having a few bottles of beer and leaving the pub sober with a girlfriend when he was sitting there like a pile of washing with the world looking down on him. There was a freedom in this knowledge too though as he realised, he didn't have much choice when he started drinking. Its like it was out with his control. Like the guy speaking said earlier, some of us had an allergic reaction to alcohol and it affected us differently. Surely that wasn't his fault? If he was allergic to something else like nuts he would stay away from them no problem, why then did the booze seem so difficult? He thought that booze done far more for him than nuts ever did. The constant panic and guilt he felt after a bender were too much now and he would do anything to put these feelings out of his life but the thought of not drinking again seemed daunting. What would he do at Christmas? Summer holidays? Nights out in toon? The football? They all seemed bland without booze. Would he manage to control his anxious mind without the help of booze slowing him down? These thoughts raced through his head a hundred mile an hour the negativity taking over any relief he felt from finding some solution in here. It was like he just wasn't allowed to stay positive. The "what if" thoughts just fucking plagued him, constantly reminding him not to get too excited or happy. Anytime he felt at ease his brain would trawl for the worst-case scenario. The meeting did uplift him a little though and he started to realise there was a wee bit more to this than just drink. He always thought that if he could deal with his drinking all would be well in his life but although he was sincere about quitting, he also felt that without booze he was raw like his armour had been taken away. It wasn't a nice place to be but he hoped he could cope without it. Frankie made a deal with himself that night. A deal that no matter what he wouldn't drink. He didn't care if he never seen the inside of another pub. He didn't care how boring life seemed. He didn't care if he had to come to more of these meetings. He didn't care how anxious he felt or what the world would think of him. He was doing this. He was going to give it his best shot. He was sick to the back teeth of how he had been living and the party was well and truly over.

A thought flashed into Frankie's mind of a time when he was at secondary school. A time of innocence. A time before all this shit muddied the water. He did have some ambition in him and he suddenly remembered that the only career he had ever shown any interest in was to be a therapist like in those movies where they help people stop drinking. He hadn't thought of that in years. Suddenly it seemed like maybe things did happen for a reason and fate was leading him down a path to where he should be. Maybe this was a new chapter and all the shit he had been through was taking him to a happier life. Not just serendipity but he had a destiny all laid out before him and every now and then he would feel like it was all taking shape. The pieces of the jigsaw were all coming together. Despite his brain telling him otherwise his gut said all would be well. Just trust the process Frankie boy. Although he had found himself at an AA meeting he just didn't feel like an alcoholic. Was his experience with drink that extreme? Did he even meet the criteria for this place if he wanted to be here? Part of him felt like a fraud. Maybe he had lived the life so long he had just accepted it for what it was. Euphoria, fear, shame, oblivion all living two millimetres under the mask he wore to get through life. He didn't want to be an alcoholic like his dad. That thought crippled him, but if he didn't make the change right now that is exactly what he would become.

He spent the next few weeks attending meetings all over Glasgow. The West End groups full of the eccentrics of the city. Tweed wearing, part time actors and writers all whom had consumed far too much booze in the four corners of the globe. Lots of guys who supported Partick Thistle. They now congregated in the coffee shops and church halls in and around Byers Road and told tales of their days of debauchery before regaining back some of their sanity. The East end was a show of tattooed men with mars bars on their wrinkled faces. Faces that had seen the inside of too many jails, mental institutions and social work offices. Although Frankie thrived at mingling with people out with his class and usual social circles, he still didn't quite feel part of. This was maybe just the familiar feeling he had felt most of his life or maybe he was in the wrong place but time would tell. He thrived on the whole honesty of the place though, he could talk about his inner world and insecurities, things he was ashamed of he had done when he was mad with it and there was no judgement here only understanding and compassion. Nobody knew an alcoholic like another alcoholic. This element kept him on the path as before when he had tried to open up about his drinking, he had felt judged and misunderstood with the people he had opened up to looking shocked or angry at him. There was none of that in these rooms. No fingers waving and he didn't need to look at his shoes when he spoke, he could be himself.

He sat in silence on a cold Wednesday night in a Parkhead church hall sooking on the polystyrene cup full of steaming coffee trying to put some heat in his bones and maybe feel something from the caffeine inside as he listened to a guy a bit younger than himself tell the story of his life before drink and what it was like now in sobriety. The story began drinking in childhood, leading to hospitals, jail cells, drink driving and psychiatric nurses. Frankie enjoyed listening and although he knew he was judging the guy he felt sorry for him in a way but hated how he was even laughing at his blackouts behind the wheel of the car. Frankie had hated drunk drivers since those adverts on the Telly where they were always killing weans.

Near the end of the guys talk Frankie felt his stomach churn a little a thought for a second, he was going to spew. The truth hit him like a sledgehammer. It was as though the curtain had been pulled up revealing his life in clearer vision. Or the static on the TV had stopped and all became a bit clearer. Frankie could see that this guy's story was so similar to his but he had somehow managed to glamorise his own story to make it seem less destructive. Less shameful. A lie he had told himself he had swallowed hook line and sinker. Frankie had begun drinking at twelve or thirteen and had rarely stopped since. He had been out of it daily for years at a time during the rave scene in the 90s. He had counted the tiles in Police Stations throughout Lanarkshire and as for the drunk driving. Never in a million year after one or two pints but after ten he was capable of anything. He had crashed twice drunk and lost the motor in blackouts more than once. His doctor had been throwing tablets at him for years in an attempt to sort him out but nothing had ever worked.

He was now convinced that not only was he in the right place but that he was far worse than most of the others in the meetings. He would sit listening to people speak and think "I have spilled more down my tie than this guy has drunk". Then he would think being an Alcoholic was the least of his worries and he had some weird mental illness which needed a label. His mind raced and raced and he changed his mind continually but every now and then he would find some clarity of thought and just knew things would get better. He would get some respite from his anxiety and his palms would stop sweating at times. Some nights he would get a decent sleep and if he was lucky the night sweats would stop now and then. The nightmares and weird dreams never left him though. It was like he had a fight set up in dreamworld and every night when he finally dropped off he would need to put his fists up and battle through another round. He would waken every morning thankful he lived to fight another day. Not knowing who or what he was fighting but it was a fight where the bell never seemed to ring and he had to keep going as his life depended on it. At least his real life was getting better. Frankie buzzed on a Monday morning now driving into work. Just having the ability to remember every bit of the previous weekend was magical to him. The fact that his wallet still contained some notes and he didn't owe a coin or an apology to anybody was enough motivation to keep him going. The weeks he was sober were gradually turning to months and finally he beat his previous record off 13 weeks off the booze. Frankie felt proud of himself. A feeling he rarely felt before but somehow, he knew he deserved it. He knew the crossroad he faced a few months ago of plodding on with the world of drink taking his life into muddier waters or turning the other way and choosing sobriety had been a moment in his life that would change things forever. He felt grateful he had chosen this path. He just hoped it was a long one.

12

Square peg - Round hole

Frankie turns the metal coin over and over between his thumb and fore finger like a catholic priest engrossed in his rosary beads. Frankie is free of worry though and he holds the coin still for a second and reads the inscription on it, "To thy own self be true" rainbowing the number 1 to represent the whole year he had stayed sober. He is beaming inside and it shows on his face. He rarely felt proud of himself, but he was proud of this. He was proud of the fact that he once struggled to get through the weekend without a drink and now he had gotten through a year without a drop passing his lips.

He buzzed off the feeling of normality in those initial months. Driving into work on a Monday morning remembering the whole weekend was magical. Sometimes it wasn't what sobriety had given him but what he had lost. The emotional rollercoaster of coming off a bender to battle with his own paranoia for his nerves to settle later in the week to start the whole process again. The constant feeling of guilt hanging over him his nerves never off high alert as though he was about to be confronted by something, someone, some imminent danger. Some of this negativity had disappeared now and other bits of it had been turned down to a manageable level. They say a fish doesn't know it's in water until you take it out. Well Frankie had been in a deep sea of thick shit for many years and he was beginning to see how he had accepted a lot of stuff that would be unacceptable to most. Stuff that he was mainly self-inflicted. He accepted the financial embarrassment, the times he made an arse of himself, the struggles going on inside his own head. Somehow though the mist was clearing as though the man he was destined to be was waking up and finally making an appearance. The knight in shining armour who had come to save him was coming from somewhere deep inside him.

Well somehow Frankie felt the stars a line. He didn't believe in any of the higher power shite he would hear some talk of in those meetings but this chapter in his life seemed meant to be somehow. Maybe there was some force orchestrating things for him but he was beginning to feel like the guy who had just crawled through miles of sewerage to get out of Shawshank. Right now, he was looking up at the sky with his hands in the air. All was well.

Well almost everything. Chucking booze was like getting rid of a crazy girlfriend you had been scared to dump for ages, you knew it was the right thing to do but it still somehow left a lonely feeling he couldn't shake at times. Never enough to run back to her though. Frankie just wasn't accustomed to the quiet life. He grew up in a madhouse, drank from a young age, the mayhem of the football, all weekend parties during the rave years and drunken blackouts made sobriety seem a little ….beige at times. He missed adventure. He missed adrenaline. He missed the gamble of throwing the dice every Friday. He was happier but still felt far from content. He once heard it described as a "hole in the soul" or a "God shaped hole needing filled". Fuck that he thought if its God shaped it can stay needing filled. The feeling of want never fully left him it was like he buzzed constantly and not just from the ten cups of coffee he consumed each day since he chucked the booze but he was beginning to realise he was always chasing a buzz or some kind of gratification.

With alcohol and drugs being a thing of the past, he focussed his attention on the other areas of his life he had gotten the most pleasure from the main one being music. Frankie had always loved music. Even from Primary School days he always had a song on loop in his head, there was always a new band he would discover and a new emotion to feel. He would spend hours in his bedroom growing up playing record after record, singing along to every word. Almost reliving the stories told in the song or feeling the heartbreak felt by the singer all way before he had experience any of the realities of life himself. Learning about life and love within the songs he grew up on had touched Frankie but also gave him a distorted view of love and relationships and anything less than Romeo and Juliet just didn't seem authentic to him. This unachievable dream had affected every relationship he had ever been in. Human beings just couldn't live up to the fantasy. Still, he loved the world that lived within the songs and he seemed to feel music deeper than most and had been a lifelong obsession but now the obsession had grown. He chased the feeling he had experienced the first time he heard "Going Underground" or the sadness of "There is a light that never goes out". He had dusted off his old Numark decks and got new needles on each turntable. He was buying records on a weekly basis. Initially he would browse the shelves in Fopp who were beginning to cotton onto the hipsters buying vinyl again before they moved onto gramophone records or some other shite to show the world how individual and superior, they were. At first, he would pick up classic albums he already owned on CD like Dark Side of The Moon, After the Goldrush, Blood on the Tracks and various other readily available bits of vinyl he could afford. As the albums piled up in his spare room he would want more and more. Some were simply bought and added to the pile and were rarely out of the sleeve. If he bought an album by say The Who he would maybe start with Quadrophenia then look at collecting all albums he considered "Mod" Who. My Generation, Sell Out, A Quick One. Then he would look at collecting sixties bands he considered Mod. The Kinks, The Small Faces, The Action, The Birds and so on. These would be stacked neatly in the section Frankie would have mentally labelled as "Mod". Then he would embark on Mod revival bands obviously beginning with The Jam, then Secret Affair, The Chords, The Purple Hearts who would all fit into his mental category of "Mod Revival". God help anybody who would return an album to the wrong section as it would shoot his anxiety to max but this was inevitable as only, he knew the unwritten system of storage all crated in his mind. It would take for him hearing one of these bands covering an old sixties R&B tune and his mind would be off on the hunt to own every classic Motown album ever released. He would rake the charity shops in the shopping precinct every lunchtime just hoping to find that 12" piece of black plastic that would provide him with the feeling he craved. The initial feeling was like a bingo winner getting all the numbers where he had a result in getting a real find for 99p. The later when the needle hit the groove back home, he could lose himself in memories of the past or create a fantasy world for himself in his mind's eye where he was the star of the show, the main character in the love story or simply The Superman to his Clark Kent. The buzz never lasted long though and he would be left with a dull feeling of longing and the chase was back on again. Sometimes he would pick up a greatest hit of someone like The Doors a band he was never fond of these days but take it because it was a bargain. Then this would open up a whole new section in the collection he would need to complete, as if on auto pilot he would be in search of all albums by The Doors including any spoken word shite by Jim Morrison who would bore him to tears with his self-indulgent drivel.

Somehow diving deep into this world of music helped fill the emptiness in Frankie a bit. If only for a short while. It gave him a focus and gave him a distraction from himself. He felt that he was living in no mans land where he was the only non-drinker in the toon who liked what he liked. Some of his old mates were his mates because they had shared interests like the football, music or whatever but they were all mostly bang at it when it came to drink and drugs and Frankie was giving them all a wide berth. The guys he had met at meetings although some were alright and great to talk to about sobriety, he just didn't have anything in common with them out with this. All which added to Frankie's feelings of being terminally unique. Although he was sure he was on the right path he just felt he wasn't ready for the pipe and slippers just yet and needed life to be a bit grittier. He needed something, anything to make the world a little brighter.

This period of his life without booze seemed to unleash a longing in him he struggled to fill. Maybe the drink was helping more than he cared to admit. Maybe it numbed something in him that was coming alive again. Something he couldn't fulfil. He spent his time drinking coffee, smoking endless cigarettes and hunting down records. Sometimes when he was out and about in the toon he would strike up conversation with females who would look like indie kids with their coloured hair and band t-shirts. Females he could easily bond with but he just couldn't muster up the courage to ask them out and anyway he felt like a total square not drinking and the prospect of any kind of date would add to his anxiety and feelings of being totally awkward. Never mind having to perform in the bedroom without any booze in him. That would be a different level of awkward. Not that Frankie was inexperienced in anyway or he felt self-conscious about his body. None of that mattered to him, but without any booze to chill him out a bit he worried if he would get a hardon? would he cum in 30 seconds flat? Would he be interested in her after the deed? Did he want some nutty woman texting him constantly or marriage on the horizon? He over thought everything and just couldn't live in the moment free of constant what if's? Maybe he should get with the times and just go on a few dates, see a movie, have dinner, go for walks. Do all the things that normal folk seemed to do on TV but that's just not how he lived. Any relationships he had in the past he met his latest flame in a pub or a nightclub or if she was really special a flat in the Scheme he had been drinking in for a few days. If it went beyond a one night stand, he would meet her second and third dates in the pub again and by that time he had found his comfort zone so there were never any issues. This living life without any Dutch courage was a new concept to him. Some of it put the frighteners up him big time. He knew it was early days though and seen himself living a life free and easy in a few months down the line he would be free of the anxiety and self-doubt. Free to live life to the full, just you wait and see.

The days when self-doubt wasn't present and his anxieties had disappeared, he would float through the day almost buzzing. When he felt free and easy his ego would inflate steadily making him feel invincible to the point of superiority. Some days he could make Liam Gallagher look like Ghandi as he strolled through the toon as if he owned the place. He had a swagger you could dry a washing on his mates would say. Frankie knew this and felt at home in this place of greatness. Though he could easily be taken down a peg with the wrong comment from someone or even a sarcastic look making him feel inferior once again and his nerves red raw. A fragile inner covered by the armour of his ego. He fooled most, including himself most of the time but to the eyes of the old he was see through. Who are you trying to kid? Was a question he had been asked by his elders on regular occasion throughout his life. A question Frankie would fail to answer. Who was he trying to kid? Why could he not just "let go" and be himself fully without the care for how others viewed him? His thought process seemed ingrained in him from way back but at times seemed illogical to him now. He would ask himself the question do I care what some arsehole in the pub thinks of me or someone in work he clashed with? He really didn't but somehow their criticism of him would still sting like throwing salt on an open wound. It was like he wasn't quite ready for the world yet he was too sensitive for it but the whole time his mask would say he didn't give a fuck. He would see bodybuilder types with shaved heads, tattooed all over marching down the street with a pit bull on a chain. The owner growling at the world more than the dog and he would think "what happened to you? You have to go through life with "Fuck off" written all over you? What are you so afraid of? It made him wonder how much of him was the mask and how much was the real Frankie? How much was any of us really showing to the world? Did we all protect ourselves under a mask of sorts. There were times when he went to church as a boy and he would watch the old women greet each other with a fake smile and false handshake rhyming off wee sayings like "it's lovely to see you" or "you're looking well" but he could see it was parrot fashion and their body language would ooze distaste. They were wearing a "nice" mask as much as the hardman was wearing a mask to cover his fragile inner. It seemed most people wanted the world to see them a certain way. Not just him. That is why ecstasy hit Scotland like a Tsunami for the first time in most people's lives they were free of any of the bullshit and could just be themselves and show the world what was going on inside them and spread the love they were so afraid to show when straight. Thankfully a wee bit of that culture stuck to some even when the drugs had worn off. For others though the hedonism of the 90s had left them were more hang ups than they started with. It seems the dream of the magic pill to solve all ills and remove any hang ups just didn't exist. Some drugs could give you a peek into another way of being but you had to find a way to get there on your own. It took courage and the strength to be an individual and Frankie was beginning to realise this but although he was out on a limb right now, he knew the good in him was trying to shine out and he would do his best to fuel the fire as much as he could.

There were nights in the flat alone he was comfortable with the solitude and would watch telly or listen to music until the early hours without a care in the world. Then other nights the loneliness would freak him out and he couldn't sit still without being tormented by thoughts of the past. Times he had made an arse of himself while he was drunk, females who had left him broken hearted, the madness of living with his father while growing up, people who had wronged him. Fuck he was pushing thirty years old and he could easily think back to school days and to a time someone had made him feel small and plot his revenge against them. It was never big events like guys he had fights with, these matters seemed done and dusted but small things that had hurt him in some way and made him look or feel small. Fleeting matters to others which stuck to him like glue. Feelings of hurt which should have been shaken off long ago. The thoughts in his head would churn over and over without any control taking him deep into the past and a focus on an old enemy. He would literally sharpen knives in his head while plotting his revenge. He would mutter to himself next time I see him… then I will… and he would play out the scene from a badly scripted Tarantino movie with some guy from 2nd year duck taped to a chair terrified at the thought of Frankie's wrath approaching. Then suddenly he would snap out of the trance as though a hypnotist clicking him back into the room and the feeling would leave him. These episodes freaked him out a bit and he would normally just try and get up and go out as though running away from himself. He never made it though. Everywhere he went, there he was right there. He knew booze could quickly turn off the dark thoughts inside him but he needed a new anaesthetic and he just hoped he would find it soon.

13

Breathe in the air

The sky was blue black and the clouds were low making the white of the clouds almost shine as day suddenly turned to night. It was a crisp night as Frankie drove the along the motorway rarely noticing another soul. It was the type of drive where you felt like the only soul in the universe. Frankie had the address on a post it note stuck to his dashboard and his eyes darted to it every few minutes reminding himself of the address he was heading towards this November night.

Frankie tried to lose himself in the long intro to Pink Floyds "Echoes" washing over him from the car stereo as he tried to prepare himself for the class. He hoped that the appointment he had made tonight would change something. Provide him with some kind of peace he longed for. Something to tell him that everything would be alright. A sign that there was a pot of gold waiting for him at the end of the rainbow and he would get his fairy tale ending. A walk off into the sunset where he would leave behind the shackles of the chains, he seemed to carry with him half his life. Since he has went to AA he had decided he was losing the chains no matter what.

In his naivety he though that when he stopped drinking within a few months he would have shaken of any negativity like it was a killer hangover and he could get on with living his life like when he was young before any real boozing. He would pick up where he had left off and take to drinking diet coke all weekend hitting pubs and clubs full of the joys and do it properly this time. Never making an arse of himself. Talk to those women who had previously intimidated him and remember every glorious moment. It had been nearly 2 years since he last had a drink and it just wasn't working out according to plan. Frankie craved the silver bullet that would make everything alright and he had hunted for it high and low over the last year or so. It seemed that spirituality was the new religion for the modern thinker and Frankie began a quest to read every self-help book known to man and made his way through the book shelves of Waterstones. He started off with the classics like "The Road Less Travelled by M. Scott Peck", "The Seven Spiritual Laws of Success" and anything else by Deepak Chopra. Then he moved onto the new age gurus and philosophers. "The Power of Now by Echhart Tolle", "The Celestine Prophecy by James Redfield". "You Can Heal Your Life, Louise Hay". Any book that referred to Buddhism or The Universal Law of Attraction would be read cover to cover. The thirst he had for self-help books almost matched the obsession he dived into when collecting records. Frankie even thought about growing his hair long and wearing a string of beads around his neck to make himself more spiritual and enlightened looking but he felt that he would be held up for ridicule so he decided against it. He had even met folk who carried crystals around with them which was meant to influence your mood. Fuck some days he would have carried dog shit in his pockets if it made him feel a little more human. He had even paid to have Reiki healing done on him which involved some middle-aged woman in a house in Hamilton holding her hands 6 inches above various parts of his body over the period of an hour which was supposed to get the energies moving again and heal any blockages. Frankie did feel better after it but he didn't know if it was maybe just because the hour in that garage was the first time he had lay still for that length of time in years. The woman who claimed she was a Reiki Master told Frankie that some Japanese guy invented Reiki after stubbing his toe and he placed his hand on the painful area and Reiki was born. This hardly filled Frankie full of confidence and the woman looked like she would have thrown in a happy ending for an extra £20.00 but he was out of there soon as. He sometimes felt that the new age folk out there knew something he didn't and was intrigued by it all but most of them he had come into contact with were the type of folk who drank water with cucumber and sat crossed legged in that trippy wee tea room in Otago Lane. Pretentious arseholes who wore Docs in the summer and talked about manifesting perfect lives. Most reminded him of those student types who were heavily into communism when they were at university but 6 months after graduation it was £50k a year, short back and sides and a bungalow in Newton Mearns. All about the image.

Now that drink and drugs were out of the picture, he needed something to help him put the brakes on a bit and time after time he had read about the Buddhist practice of meditation. Frankie knew very little about meditation but it conjured up images of crossed legged monks sitting on mountain tops in silence for days at a time. An image that didn't really appeal to him much but he knew he had his back against the wall here. He once spoke to a guy in a meeting who waxed lyrical about the benefits of meditation and how it had changed his life and how he felt. Apparently, the guy found it in Barlinnie when he shared a cell with some hippy guy who was doing time for bringing vast quantities of cannabis to Bonnie Scotland. He told Frankie how initially he felt he was unable to relax a little and even close his eyes for long in fear of the guy attacking him when trying to meditate but after he kept at it he says he found a peace in Barlinnie like he never knew on the outside and the practice had stuck with him ever since and had helped him stay clean of drink and drugs. Frankie always raised a smile when he pictured the two "ohmmin" away in the cell looking for inner peace. Maybe it could work for him too.

That Buddhist place was just off Woodlands Road and he was welcomed by a guy who told him he was one of the Monks there. Frankie fired questions at the guy machine guy style about meditation, a retreat maybe, could he buy beads? The guy was friendly enough but suggested Frankie take it one step at a time and maybe come into the beginner's class that night?

Frankie agreed and thought what did he have to lose? The Monk who took the class was dressed in jeans and a t-shirt and looked very normal. The class of maybe 15 were of all different shapes and sizes and nothing too weird about it. There was herbal tea on the go though. The monk began to explain a little about the nature of the mind and how it would constantly look for thoughts to latch onto and would constantly be in a state or planning or remembering. Rarely in the moment. With the practice of meditation, we could find the present moment and experience life with full attention. He then went onto pass a puma stone round the class. A stone like the one your granny would use to scrub all the dead skin off her feet. A wee grey stone which was rough and ragged. The Monk asked each individual to actually feel the stone and describe its texture etc. This would help take the class to the present moment. He then spoke about a similar practice while eating food and trying to actually taste the food, maybe put down your knife and fork between mouthfuls and chew it properly. Be mindful of what you were eating. This intrigued Frankie as he had always eaten very fast, always first finished and he thought he would try this next time he ate. The monk then guided the class through a 20-minute meditation which he called "a body scan". It involved taking your attention to each body part starting at your feet and then releasing the tension you were holding there and letting it all go. After the 20-minute Frankie felt light, relaxed, unafraid. A feeling that was alien to him in life unless he had taken Valium. It was exactly what he needed.

After the class Frankie chatted more to the Monk guy who told him he had been practicing meditation for many years as he was also in recovery from a heroin habit he had developed in the eighties in London. The guy was a windae cleaner by day and a Monk at night! He was just a normal guy who had found some peace through the Buddhist teachings. Frankie liked the sound of it all.

He left the centre that night buzzing inside, buzzing that he may have found the missing piece to the puzzle that may make him whole. As though he had finally found the answer. This feeling of hope was also fairly strange to him but he knew he had made a break through that night and another door had open to him.

The endless books he had been reading and his visits to the meditation class gave Frankie a little more insight into himself, the idea that he might be able to put his experience to good use and maybe help others made him want to explore this. He might even make a few quid along the way he thought. Frankie had grown up in a very male dominated world and he had embraced the madness of alcohol and violence from an early age but maybe he was kidding himself a little. Maybe he wasn't the alpha male after all maybe he should be more honest with himself about his sensitive side. Not only that Frankie was beginning to realise that pretending to be hard all the time and that you didn't give a fuck wasn't that easy. He had justified his anxieties in the past by telling himself that it was just a side effect of his "Rock & Roll" lifestyle. A badge of honour that he had partied harder than most, but he hadn't partied for a long time now and he felt more anxious some days. He lived his life like a firework in a phone box. Constantly in 5th gear. When he finally managed to get out of bed in the morning it was full steam ahead. He brushed his teeth in the shower with one hand while washing his hair with the other. He drove to work 100 miles an hour and ate breakfast as he drove. When he was clocking in he wanted to be on the morning fag break. At lunchtime he inhaled his food while planning that night's dinner. He was always a step ahead of himself planning, planning, planning. If he wasn't looking to the future he thought of the past in dread or disgust but he was never in the moment. Ever. He would get to bed at night mentally and physically exhausted but just couldn't switch his head off and sleep would always be a struggle. The adrenaline pumped through his veins every minute of the day and he rarely felt relaxed. His high levels of anxiety all his life had added to his sensitivities and perfectionism and truth be told being him for a day was fuckin hard work!

The next few nights Frankie lit a few candles in his living room and tried to set the scene in the same way he would during his dope smoking days except now he was trying to do this naturally. He sat on the chair with his back straight and attempted to slow his mind down to a riot. He followed the instructions the windae cleaner had shown him and tried to breath in slowly through his nose, taking his breath deep into his stomach and back out again. When his mind began to wander, he would try and take his attention back to his breath again taking him to the place beyond thought where stillness lived just like the guy told him. "This is easy", "My tooth aches", "whits on the telly", "I fuckin hate him", "I want a vespa", "My whole body is buzzin", back to the breath again. Breathe in really, really slow and out really slow. "Be here now" he told himself, "Be here now" was that an Oasis album? "I liked Blur better" and breathe in. He looked at his watch and 6 minutes had passed and he must have counted three or four breaths the rest of the time his brain just ran a tape on auto showing him images of anything and everything. From what he wants for dinner, females, school, work tomorrow, he must remember and Iron a shirt etc etc. Not as easy as it looked finding inner peace. He was starting to realise for the first time the state his mind could get it and how much his head ruled him.

He thought tea lights and breathing in his flat might not be cutting it for him so he may need to buy a few more books, maybe get some matts for the floor, those beads they hold with the orange feathers and maybe sandals. In fact, he decided he would take more classes, no fuck that he would go on a mountain retreat for a few months and maybe take a career break. He would come back with a shaved head, detoxed, clear skinned and cooler than penguin piss. Let's do it!

14

Slaying the Dragon

That feeling of want, dimmed a little but never really left Frankie. The knot in his stomach was forever present though bothered him far less. Not having the shite in his life that came with alcohol was well worth the struggles in sobriety but he still craved contentment and felt that he should be happier as the time passed by. He developed an attitude that after six months he would have no anxiety. Twelve months he would be content and confident. Year two he would be zen like etc etc but it just wasn't panning out as he planned. He could go weeks feeling happy and fairly content then get low days, anxious days, sleepless nights. There was no real constant in his mood and some of the old thinking of dreading impending doom never fully left him. The exercise and meditation were helping but he was beginning to think that this twelve-step programme that they talked about in meetings might be for him after all as everything else he had done in AA so far had done him good. When he read the steps hanging up on display in meetings, he quickly wrote them off in his mind as it seemed to be all about God and he didn't want to be one of those crack pots who gave up the drink and started quoting the bible. Some of the guys who preached about the steps seemed far too intense for him and had some aura of superiority about them. It was as though their time in recovery had made them super human. It held very little appeal to him. It was as though they had merely swapped the mask, they had worn in their drinking days as the local hard man or womaniser to this new cleaner mask of an evangelist. Over egging the pudding that they had changed. Frankie was sick of masks and just wanted to be comfortable with himself. He felt that his old self wasn't all bad and he just wanted to weed out the bad bits of himself not be rubbed out and drawn back in again as some perfect wanker. The guys that were always banging on about the twelve steps seemed to brow beat themselves for every negative though or emotion they experienced as though they would go to hell if they got a hardon. Frankie felt he had some potential in him, there was a lot of good in him and though over analysing things would only add to his anxieties and dim the self-belief he had but he was still far from content and was thinking maybe this was for him after all despite the God thing putting him off a bit.

He had recently had coffee after the meeting with a guy called Michael who had been sober for a few years and had gone through the process of the twelve steps and Frankie liked Michael. He seemed like a normal guy who could talk about normal stuff and was not obsessed about recovery like some. Michael had a good way about him that Frankie was drawn to. A guy who lived life free of alcohol and drugs but still enjoyed much of the stuff he did previously like football or music and seemed to have his shit together a bit. This was all Frankie was really looking for and the idea that he would develop into some new age monk in recovery had long since left him in favour of normality.

The issue with God was still there though and although church had been a regular Sunday affair as a boy, he had always felt that it just wasn't for him and that no way was there a God up in heaven. The idea seemed ludicrous to him and a concept well outdated. Even as a child he didn't believe in shite about Noah's Ark and attending church just made him feel like a snob in comparison to all his other friends as he knew very few protestants who actually went to church. While most were obsessed with hating Catholics for some reason. It baffled him.

As Frankie got to know Michael more, he felt he would give it a go and Michael agreed to help Frankie go through the process which would help him clear up the wreckage of the past and live happier in the present. Ideal Frankie thought while worrying what people would think about him doing this God shite.

It surprised him however when he got into it with Michael when they looked at the impact alcohol had had on Frankie's life and how much it had affected him from an early age. His Fathers alcoholism and the impact it had had on his whole life with a feeling of being on the outside looking in hanging over him since primary school. The other kids in his class mostly seemed well adjusted compared to him but they weren't going home to the house he was living in. He had been living in an atmosphere awaiting the next attack for the majority of his life. His mother had simply clammed up during all his Fathers madness leaving him with feelings of being all alone in the world with nobody to turn to. He began to see how the booze had given him something he lacked in life. A comfort he just didn't have naturally. It explained his constant feeling of impending doom. His need for connection caused him to seek attention from people when all he really wanted was to feel part of in a world, he felt alone in. His relationships with women had been unhealthy as his self-worth just wasn't there under the act, he had perfected to seem not only on top of things but above everyone. He cared too much of what everyone thought of him. The fear of what others thought drove his every action. Michal explained that this was some of the stuff that he had to change or he would repeat the same behaviour over and over again. He had to find his self-worth and be an equal in any relationship not play second fiddle or try to control women. Frankie began to see how he wanted women high on the looks department and not just to satisfy his sexual desires but to gave him some comfort that he wouldn't be ridiculed and the better looking the female added to his ideas of how others seen him. It gave him a better place in the pecking order. It all seemed bonkers when he read what he had written for Michael. Bonkers but it began to make sense that he had to change. A lot of his issues were simply not part of reality but came from the fact that he spent far too much time in his own head.

Step eight and nine of the programme involved making a list of people who he had harmed and making amends to them where he could. Frankie didn't feel that he had a million apologies to make as he had always felt despite the macho image, he tried to project he was just too soft for the world. He felt the world had been unkind to him not the other way around. It pissed him off when

Michael smiled and wanted Frankie to have a second look. Jesus he thought this guy would have the Jews apologising to the fuckin Nazis. There were some patterns he couldn't deny though most relationships he had been in Frankie found it difficult to say how he felt and would end them without any real explanation and had hurt a few women along the way without even realising it. He felt justified at the time as he has always felt used by them during the relationship. He realised he had some work to do. The prospect of looking up old girlfriends terrified him as he had generally avoided bumping into ex's at all costs. He would go to great lengths to stay out of their way to avoid any uncomfortable questions or have them tell him how well they were doing without him. Avoidance was his default setting and now he had to find the strength to face up to his faults. It made sense to him as it might stop him looking down the isles in Asda to see who was about before he walked down them. It would be nice to relieve his paranoia a wee bit.

Over a few weeks he made a few uncomfortable phone calls in an attempt to clear up the wreckage of the past. He had to eat large chunks of humble pie explaining that he was trying to change his ways and had stopped drinking etc etc etc. One or two were a wee bit dry with him but on a whole, he got a decent response and felt he had done his best to make good. The load he had been carrying on his shoulders was getting lighter and he did start to feel free in some ways. The cloud left over from his drinking days was being lifted. He could feel it. He worked his way down the list until he came to one he dreaded. His old man. Should he really be apologising to this old bastard? Okay he did attack him and it had bothered him then, but time had past and Frankie had begun to justify it to himself. Should he no be apologising to me for his behaviour not the other way around? Michael explained that the resentment he carried for his father was poison to him and it would be the number one cause for him drinking again if he didn't deal with it. He understood that Frankie had been a victim in many ways but this was about his side of the street not his fathers. It seemed there was no exceptions if he wanted to do this sincerely, he would have to speak to his father and say sorry.

It had been over two years since that night his father had felt Frankie's rage and he hadn't laid eyes on him since and there had been no visits from the police or come backs of any kind. This spoke volumes to Frankie but he had still been in the wrong. He planned on visiting his old man after work that Monday. Monday came and went and Frankie promised it would be Tuesday, then Wednesday. He finally got sick of the thought hanging over him and went there that Thursday after work knocking on the door hoping there would be no answer. Just as he was about to turn on his heals and leave, he heard the key turn in the lock and the door opened. The two looked at each other straight in the eye for what seemed like an eternity before Frankie muttered can I speak to you for a minute? Without speaking his father nodded for him to come in and walked down the hall towards the living room. The smell of chip pan oil and smoke hit Frankie as he walked into the old family home. The carpet was thick with dust and there were bin bags filled with rubbish everywhere.

The living room looked like it hadn't seen a hoover since his Mum had died and the atmosphere in the room was as thick as the dust. His father sat in his usual armchair uttering for Frankie to sit down. The prospect of sitting on the pish stained couch revolted Frankie but he had a job to do so sat anyway. They went through the uncomfortable formalities of how you doing before Frankie began his well-rehearsed speech. He told his old man that he had stopped drinking and realised that the night he had attacked him he was well out of order and wanted to apologise. He knew he was in the wrong. His old man said nothing but nodded as Frankie spoke sensing his discomfort. There was an uncomfortable silence and Frankie rose to leave when his father suddenly spoke. "I'm glad you have stopped drinking son and you are doing alright. I wish I had stopped it years ago it has caused me nothing but misery, look after yourself." Not the most profound statement he had ever heard but it meant a lot to Frankie. There were few words spoken between the two but the air had been cleared somehow and there seemed to be some kind of understanding. Frankie fought back the tears as he said, "Thanks Dad," and left. He cried like a baby during the short drive home and the knot in his stomach disappeared. His old man had become human, not a monster but a man. A man who Frankie had hated for most of his life suddenly seemed vulnerable and alone. A man to feel compassion for not hate. He had hated enough. It was over now time to move on.

Every amends he made he felt better and felt he could easily knock it on the head now as he was beginning to feel redeemed and pure. Clean enough to live the good life.

That wouldn't be true though there was still one niggle in the back of his mind. One niggle that would haunt him from time-to-time. Fat Boy.

Fat Boy from Rangers was walking around with a scarred face because of what Frankie had done to him. Did Fat boy deserve an apology? or did he accept it was all part of the game and he should accept his lot? He played about with this though. Years had passed since then true but what impact the scarring have on Fat Boys life? He knew that if the roles were reversed Frankie would plot his revenge night after night alone in bed. Did Fat Boy do the same or was he made of sterner stuff and had let it go years ago? Maybe Fat Boy had given it out many times and Frankie was Fat Boys karma? He decided if this was no big deal, he wouldn't even be talking about it and he couldn't deny that he felt bad for what he had done. For months after that game, he felt he would be jumped at some point and left like a teabag. He would need to try to contact Fat Boy somehow. It would be the last piece of the past Frankie needed to clear up and he would accept his fate. He felt it unlikely that Fat Boy would shake hands and walk away, he might want to cut Frankie to even up the score. Give him a taste of his own medicine. Frankie would need to prepare for this. Maybe he would speak to Michael before he made contact. This would need to be played properly or could all blow up in his face. Maybe a phone call rather than face to face would be best here.

It was well known that a Rangers boy had been ripped that day after the match, there were many stories to tell of football over the years. There had been times where he had even enjoyed the notoriety attached to the story which would be brought up in conversation time and time again. It had ensured Frankie's place in the casual hall of fame but he knew he didn't deserve any of it. He was one unfortunate guy who did give a fuck.

Frankie knew that one of the Rangers lads had a clothes shop in town and was making a living out of selling clobber and had given up the football long ago. Frankie had been in there once or twice and had kept himself under the radar but got a feeling this guy was alright and might be able to help out. That Saturday Frankie parked outside the shop waiting for his opportunity for when the shop would be empty. He took his chance and went inside browsing the rails, faking interest while he waited on his moment. He felt strangely calm as though knowing doing something righteous for once, things were going to work out. He exchanged small talk with the guy who wasn't that much older than him, commenting on the jackets and sweatshirts on display and how nice they were. Frankie directed the conversation suddenly asking the guy if he used to be Rangers? The two began exchanging war stories and dropped names of faces from all over Scotland. This stuff was second nature to them both. This was their comfort zone. Frankie seized the opportunity to bring up the match where the guy got ripped at the civic?

Instantly the guy knew of the day and the two elaborated on the story and who done what to who? Frankie then asked who was the big guy who got ripped?

"Paul Jones… God rest him." God rest him! What is he deid?

It seems Fat Boy was one of the original ICF for Shettleston. Rangers through and through. Had been there from day one. Paul had lived his life through Rangers then like many others had gotten into Heroin, it had taken about two years until he faded away and his life was over. He had died of an overdose at only twenty-eight years of age.

Frankie felt for Fat Boy but also felt some relief at the same time, relief that had faced this and found the truth.

The following week he phoned The Council pretending he was a long-lost relative visiting back home from abroad who wanted to pay his respects to Mr Jones. He noted the address of the East End graveyard and planned a visit to Paul. Frankie felt that he still owed him something. His death wouldn't be a get out of jail card for Frankie. He trawled round and round the graveyard until he found the headstone. Paul Jones 1971 – 1999 "Simply the Best". He knelt by the tiny grave stone and told Paul he was sorry for what he done to him and that he hoped he was at peace. He meant it. Before Frankie left he went into his pocked and brough out the metal chip he had gotten when he reached one year sober. He left it at the grave side reading the inscription on the chip one last time. "To thy own self be true". Walking away he promised himself and Paul that he would try to be a better man. He hoped his sobriety could at least make up for Paul's loss in the world of addiction. Frankie knew he had a chance here that many never. He would make the most of it.

15

Time is on my side

The two locked eyes for a few seconds before they both looked away. One knowing his lies had fell on deaf ears the other seeing straight through the transparent bullshit his opponent spouted. Frankie sat cross legged in the small, dimly lit counselling room. He felt that familiar feeling of superiority, safe in the knowledge he was firmly in the driving seat and would steer this just as he pleased. It was territory he could navigate through blindfolded. The notepad he held was merely a prop in this instance as there would be little need for him to analyze any of this self-absorbed delusion being shat all over him. They would get to the truth soon but for now he was happy to keep up the pretense and indulge young Christopher who sat in front of him. Frankie knew Christopher well yet they had only spent a few hours in each other's company. Frankie used to be young Christopher.

A young man lost in the world, a world created by a troubled mind and a need to belong to something. Like Frankie, Christopher was looking in all the wrong places. Staring down to the bottom of too many bottles and desperately trying to fill the void inside with powder, pills and betting slips. Anything to relieve him of the uneasy feeling he struggled to live with. He had bought into that lie that at the end of the rainbow there was a pot of gold with his name on it. A pot of gold that would cure him and make it all alright. Frankie knew the drill only too well here but Christopher was a million miles away from seeing the truth. Frankie hoped he could help him get there and keep him alive. It still baffled Frankie at how normal this life was is Scotland, why so many held onto drink with both hands when their lives were in tatters with it. Did it make you less of a man if you didn't take a drink? Were you seen as soft or some sort of weirdo? Never trust a man who doesn't take a drink he once heard his father tell him.

Some of these values seemed old fashioned to him now. When men were men it seems, hardworking, covered in dirt, breaking their backs for pennies. Unopened wage packets handed into the wife on a Friday and hell to be paid if they weren't. Saturday was for the drink to forget the mundane life and Sunday to deal with the shame of Saturday. Men who could talk little more than football and horses. Don't show feelings that's for poofs.

Then the next generation like young Christopher sitting here in front of him wondering why he felt unloved? Only one run up the ladder of evolution than his father but with more money than his father and grandfather could only have dreamt of but nothing much to contribute. The cocaine epidemic fed off young blood like Christopher.

The session ended and Christopher left with a mere peek at the truth. It would be a long while before he could take off his mask and hopefully be one of the lucky ones who would make it. So many just accepted life. Nothing ever changed.

It had been fifteen years since Frankie had last had a drink. The fifteen years had flown in. His hair was greying and his waistline expanding but he knew he was one of the lucky ones. He had made it. He had gotten out. He was conditioned from the word go to embrace drink, hold it up like something to cherish. The golden potion where happiness lay. He had bought into it hook, line and sinker, creating a life for himself which revolved around the stuff. Drink began as something that made you grown up, then it became something that he equated as the fun part of life. Everything else so dull in comparison. In no time at all the dullness outside drink was hard to bear and the shine drink once provided just wasn't there any longer. What a shit place to be. A place he had fought hard to get out of and would keep fighting with his last breath.

Frankie finally seen through the illusion he had created from himself. There was little reality in the drinking world. He had stuck with that deal he made with himself that no matter how bad life got he wouldn't put another drop past his lips. In early years he simply didn't want to go back to feel how drink had made him feel about himself but as time moved on his motivation changed. He now felt he was worth more than drink. He was worth more than being the court jester in some shitty boozer. He was worth more than feeling less than. He found a fire inside him and he stocked the flames. Found out what he was good at and had worked hard at building a new life.

He kept working with the council for a few years enjoying just living a normal life, making it into work on time, no more phoning in sick. The Monday club went on without him. Speaking in AA had taught him something about himself. That he was good at some stuff. He was actually good at expressing himself, listening to other folk. He had a natural way of understanding people and people seemed to be drawn to him to ask for help. One day he got sick of listening to himself talking about the future and just bit the bullet and applied to go to night school at Glasgow University. It terrified him and excited him at the same time. He was going to Uni. Could he talk the talk with the normal folk out there who weren't in recovery or would he be overwhelmed by that old feeling of being on the outside looking in? Fuck it he thought he was going to try.

He loved the class from the word go. Looked forward to every Thursday night. He had a good rapport with his fellow students and most had been attracted to learning counselling skills as they all had a story to tell. Some of them struggled in the first few weeks and never came back. Frankie was determined he was going to succeed. It made him realize he wasnt so different after all. He once though the world around him had its shit together and he was the only one struggling, he was beginning to realize this had been another lie. Just because you don't need alcohol or drugs to get through doesn't mean you are the finished article with no issues. He began to see himself as fortunate, fortunate that he had the ability to pinpoint his issues and identify what needed fixed. He had a game plan. It made him laugh when he watched some of the girls in his class trying to fix themselves with sunbeds, make up, handbags, BMWs, boyfriends. His favorite ones were new age lot who felt their anxiety was caused because they were just too empathic and had been sent here to be energy guides or some other shit. Just wearing the dreadlocks in the same way, the others wore Gucci. Nobody was ready to admit they were afraid or mummy and daddy had fucked them up. AA had allowed Frankie to get real. His story was transparent now. Living in an alcoholic home had damaged him as a child. He didn't feel connected to anyone or anything and sought connection through being an attention seeker from primary school. Tried to make the casuals his family, and they were in a weird way. He did feel part of things there. The constant attacks from his old man had made relaxation a foreign concept to him he had to find peace in chemical form. It was text book stuff. He wasn't that different to many others. He wasn't just a recovering alcoholic, he was recovering from trauma. He realized he had to spend the last part of his life recovering from the past. He did the work to rebalance himself and sort out his over active nervous system. He finally began to see he had a shot at life. He could achieve the things that others could, better sometimes but he only every tried to be better than the man he was yesterday and go forward one day at a time. It was working. He passed the first course with flying colours and it boosted his confidence giving him a hunger for more. He signed up for the next course straight away and read book after book on counselling, psychiatry, mental health. He felt he knew some of this stuff instinctively. It helped him understand not only himself but the behavior of others too. He seen where people had been jealous in the past and he though they disliked him for no reason. He could now see the defects and cracks in others. It made the fear he once carried of what others thought of him just vanish.

With more qualifications under his belt, he started volunteering part time in a local rehab facility counselling men and women who were new to recovery. The work fed his soul somehow. It boosted his self-worth and made him feel good that he was helping others too. Within a couple of years, he had chucked the council and had never looked back working full time in the rehab. He didn't rest on his laurels though he kept studying until he was able to practice on his own. He counselled all sorts of people from alcoholics, addicts, anorexics, people with PTSD. He had finally found his niche in life. Something he was actually good at. He even got some counselling himself, allowed himself to feel for the first time and not run away from himself like he had always done. Tears were shed and the burdens he carried were lighter and lighter until he carried them with ease.

In the early years he rarely seen some of his old mates as they kept living in the boozers. Some he tried to hold onto but he could feel the bad vibes as they didn't like the new Frankie. He had boundaries now, no longer a joke figure. One by one he found the courage to walk away from the people who held him back. Tommy was still around. Tommy had been his best mate since school. Tommy understood Frankie and was happy for him. The two old mates spoke on the phone and still went to the odd game but most of their time spent together was climbing hills on Sundays. They had climbed Ben Lomond one summer just to see what all the fuss was about and in no time at all they had gotten all the gear and had been all over Scotland bagging hill after hill. They had been through a lot together over the years and they were men now. Sometimes it felt like they were almost grown up.

It used to frustrate him when he seen the bright lights of the pubs and clubs at the weekend and he would feel lonely and envy those still living the old life. He felt he was destined to live alone in his wee flat forever. He had rebuilt his confidence but still struggled to ask women out on a date. He had never really done the dating thing. He had always introduced himself to females while drunk and sometimes it grew from there other times it went nowhere. Where would he even ask someone out? In Asda? In the gym? It all seemed like hard work to him and pretty pointless. He finally plucked up the courage to go on a few dates here and there but it just felt awkward to him. Sitting in coffee shops and restaurants interviewing each other about likes and dislikes. It all felt forced and false. He felt square not drinking, it was like he would either be a non-drinking hard working guy who was beige all over or he would tell them a bit about his past to make himself seem less boring and they would avoid him like the plague there after. He just didn't fit into the straight world and his old life was dead. It was a bit of a no mans land for a while.

Something changed when he met Tricia. He was on some training course through work and he liked her straight away. The two just clicked. Hit it off and had a laugh. When the course ended that day there was no awkward feeling or shyness, he simply had to see her again. He didn't even know if she was single at this point and almost rugby tackled her as they left the class to get her phone number. She gave him it without hesitation and he buzzed that day as he left her, something inside him knew he was meant to meet her. The two text obsessively for a week winding each other up, sharing bits of their lives. When they met the following weekend, it was like he had known her forever. They were inseparable from day one. She was the first person he had ever met where he could be fully himself and be at ease with. There was never any judgement from her. She liked the fact that he didn't drink and was trying hard to better himself. She seen it for what it was, a good thing. Not something to judge him about. They had both lived a bit of life and she had been out with men before who had put drink before her every time and she knew there was a better life. A life Frankie could give. After a year he moved out of the flat and they bought a house together. A house Frankie would have seen out of his league when he was growing up. Right in the middle of spam valley. Their house was happy, peaceful even. It took him a bit of getting used to. He seen peace as boring before but it was exactly what he craved at the same time. He would pinch himself sometimes and worry when the shit was going to hit the fan. When was he going to lose his job? When would Tricia leave him? Was there a chap at the door coming with bad news? He fought against the negative though and his securities began to win over his insecurities. He just thought "fuck it whatever happens I can handle it". He just got sick of being worried and started letting stuff go.

The two had travelled all over, places he would never have seen before, Italy, America, France, Canada, Jamaica. It made him see more and more how Scotland had shaped him particularly when it came to booze. He could unlearn a lot of that stuff, it was out with his control when he was growing up. He chose how he lived now and he would live well. The love he shared with Tricia made him feel almost whole. It was something he lacked growing up. Now he had found it and it was real. They didn't play games with each other and looked after each other. He felt like as he levelled up, he attracted better into his life. Looking back on his previous relationships the females were all as messed up as he was. It started making sense that he was pairing up with the damaged and the sick. He was like that. Maybe there was something this new age bullshit about attraction after all.

The mundane life was something he felt he would have to settle for in sobriety but it seems he was wrong. His world got bigger not smaller. He had so many varied types of people in his circle, had seen so many places and had the cash to do what he pleased. He began to enjoy the moment, his head was no longer ten steps ahead of him. He was no longer driven by fear but by joy. He seen the world as somewhere to be explored and life as a path he walked which opened up in front of him revealing more and more to him. He was able to achieve stuff and finally felt equal to his fellow man. He no longer had anybody on pedestals or looked down his nose at them.

The nightmares he had had since he was young kept happening. He still fought that wee boy every other night, over and over they would roll about. Frankie would still wake in the morning saturated in sweat having fought hard in his dreamworld. One night Frankie faced the wee boy square on. He felt calm as if the two knew the time had come. Frankie reached out and grabbed the schoolboy by the throat and held him still with all his strength. He used his right fist to smash the child's face time after time like a jack hammer. When he finally let him go, he got up and ran from Frankie. He ran into the night and Frankie never seen him again. It was though some curse had finally been broken and he had slept in peace every night since.

Conclusion

Although Frankie's story is a work of fiction there are many similarities to not only my own life but to many of my friends and to those I have met along the way. Scotland's relationship with alcohol is well known and drink is heavily ingrained in our culture. Many of us are exposed to unhealthy relationships with alcohol from a very young age and begin the quest to become part of that culture when we are just stepping out of childhood. This was a cultural norm and excess was celebrated and encouraged during the era I grew up in. The current Cocaine epidemic we are facing has only added to the issue with mental health issues on the increase and sadly suicide in young men a regular occurrence.

I personally drank for fifteen or sixteen years of my life

knocking the booze on the head when I was twenty-nine years of age. To have drunk for that period of time is way beyond experimentation or simply deciding drink wasn't for me. There were many good times in the early days when drink was merely a social lubricant and I enjoyed the drinking culture initially following football, and nights out in the town like many of us do. I have many memories of days I wouldn't change during my youth.

I later felt a frustration comparing myself to others who seemed to continue to enjoy alcohol and maintain a normal life while personally, I was unable to put drink down when I started drinking and I struggled with high levels of anxiety and my self-esteem. Some of these changes in my drinking and how I felt crept up on me over a period of years and I was unaware of the progression until I was hurting enough to change. Meanwhile many others maintained a healthy lifestyle and social drinking. We are not all the same when it comes to alcohol.

I came to realize that I would have been unable to deal with any of these issues until I tackled the main issue for me which was drink. I learnt the differences between people like myself and social drinkers. I had to accept that alcohol affected me and those like me in a different way and that when I consumed alcohol, I set up a craving for more and more. My thirst for alcohol could never be quenched once I had started drinking. This affect does not happen to every drinker and some of us take it to the depths of insanity trying to prove to themselves they can drink socially.

This realisation and acceptance was a massive benefit to me and I no longer consume alcohol in any form, however I then had to face the adult world without the benefit of any anesthetic. The path into living sober was euphoric in the initial months and cutting alcohol out of my life was like ending a toxic relationship. I loved remembering the previous evening every morning when I woke to face a new day. I no longer had the Monday blues or any paranoia at the beginning of each week. My financial situation improved greatly as I no longer spend the vast majority of my hard-earned cash in pubs and clubs.

As life progressed in recovery some of the old feelings of self-doubt and bouts of anxiety would return and I learned that these negative feelings and emotions were not only side effects of my previous life style but also part of my make-up due to years of conditioning. I had to make changes to tackle my negative emotions and characteristics. Initially this involved practical stuff that many would take for granted such as restoring some sort of normal sleeping pattern as I had previously gone days each week without sleep or binged on sleep mid-week. I ceased consuming massive amounts of caffeine each day in an attempt to rebalance my nervous system as many problems drinkers substitute alcohol for coffee, tea or energy drinks in early recovery. Similar to sleep I had to restore a healthy eating pattern as I again would fail to eat for days and binge eat mid-week. This had a big impact on blood sugar and my mood which helped increase energy levels naturally.

Exercise became a part of weekly routine as it helped

burn off any nervous energy and gave my serotonin a regular boost. These practical steps were very beneficial to me and to how I felt day to day.

There are many studies now shown that those suffering from addiction may also suffer from dopamine deficiency and without the user's drug of choice their mood may be lower than that of an individual with healthy dopamine levels. It is important to keep the feel-good chemicals in the body high through exercise or other practices such as yoga. The key here though is to find a suitable balance as many of us in recovery can take exercise to extremes. I feel the middle ground works best for me.

Although many of us in recovery share many similar traits, we are all individuals and each of us will carve out their own brand of recovery. Some recover quicker than others depending on the action they take to recover or the challenges they face in life. Some of us have greater traumas to overcome from their past while living sober.

Rebuilding my self-esteem began with ceasing the drunken behavior as behaving out of character or making an exhibition of yourself over many years of drinking can have a massive impact on your self-image and how the world views you. Some toxic friendships or relationships had to end as I was impacted greatly by the company I kept and like tends to attract like and many of my old acquaintances were people who lived very similar to how I did. At times this was not easy and I had to find the courage to be disliked by some if necessary and lose my old fears of what the world thought of me. My relationships with others became healthier but it relied on me having healthier boundaries and becoming more assertive with expressing myself and how I felt. This was always a challenge initially but as my self-esteem grew people got used to the new me and being assertive became second nature.

Alcoholism and dysfunction in families can cause a great deal of damage in childhood and I understand now that I was greatly affected by alcoholism from a young age which caused me to view the world through the eyes of someone who was always hyper vigilant with a hyper aroused nervous system. I was sensitive because of this and my fight or flight mode was always switched on. Relaxation without chemical assistance was something I had to learn. I had to develop a healing lifestyle which means maintaining my sobriety, practicing meditation and generally looking after my mind and body. Through writing this book I have also discovered the fulfilment to be found in creativity. My hope is that Frankie's story may inspire the reader to reflect on their relationship with alcohol and maybe like me you will realize that there is another way of living despite our cultural conditioning in relation to booze. I once felt I did not qualify for attendance of twelve step followships as I did not drink daily and still had a roof over my head etc but the truth is alcohol and recreational drug use had a serious detrimental effect on my life and there is no need for anyone to take it to the end of the line before stopping. We each have our own story and it doesn't have to include the extremities of prison cells or rough sleeping before we can change. I will be forever grateful for my sobriety and the help I received from twelve step fellowships as I found recovery was near impossible without help. I can't we can!

Available worldwide from Amazon

Michael Terence Publishing

www.mtp.agency

www.facebook.com/mtp.agency

@mtp_agency